TROUBLE AT TENKILLER

Also by Ray Hogan
in Thorndike Large Print ®

Renegade Gun
The Bloodrock Valley War
Solitude's Lawman

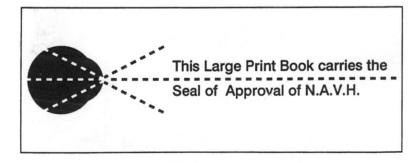

This Large Print Book carries the
Seal of Approval of N.A.V.H.

TROUBLE AT TENKILLER

Ray Hogan

LT
W
HOGAN
c.1

Thorndike Press • Thorndike, Maine

Library of Congress Cataloging in Publication Data:

Hogan, Ray, 1908-
  Trouble at tenkiller / by Ray Hogan.
    p. cm.
  ISBN 1-56054-575-5 (alk. paper : lg. print)
  1. Large type books. I. Title.
  [PS3558.O3473T76   1993]   92-36434
  813'.54—dc20   CIP

Thorndike Large Print® Western Series edition published
in 1993 by arrangement with Donald MacCampbell, Inc.

Cover photo by Thayer Smith.

The tree indicium is a trademark of Thorndike Press.

This book is printed on acid-free, high opacity paper. ∞

TROUBLE AT TENKILLER

I

The old Diamond-Stack labored up the final grade, chuffing industriously, wheels clanking noisily as it belched smoke into the afternoon air. There were only two coaches, one for passengers, the other for freight, but the locomotive was worn and weary and the climb to the rim overlooking Tenkiller Flats was steep.

When they reached the summit Dave Keegan would be able to see the settlement, Cabezon, with its collection of weathered buildings, low-roofed houses and single, dusty street. He wondered if it had grown during the ten years he had been away, then decided such was unlikely. Towns like Cabezon changed little during the passage of time.

From the rim he would be able to see other things, too: the towering Tenkiller Mountains lifting in shadowed majesty beyond the valley; the broad, sage green flats that flowed from them in seemingly limitless undulations; Wolf River, a bright, jagged slash cutting diagonally across the land on its way to join the Rio Grande.

A hard-jawed man with quiet eyes, his features softened as he gave that thought. There he had been born, had grown, attended school and finally at fifteen, unable to further abide his father after the death of his mother, had taken his leave. But there were good memories, as well as bitter ones and often at night as he lay near the fire in some lonely cow camp, Dave Keegan thought back over the years and wondered if he had done right.

He guessed there was no way of really knowing. He had taken to the trails; Sam Keegan had stayed to run his ranch in the manner he thought best. Therein had lain the bone of contention. Pride Seevert, owner of the vast Seven Diamond spread, had proposed a combine of ranches on the Flats — a syndicate in which he, by virtue of size and power, would be the head. Outwardly it was a voluntary organization, but those who opposed Pride and his two brothers soon found themselves under brutal persuasion.

To Dave's young mind it had appeared only a variation of peonage and he'd taken no pains to hide his opinions; Sam Keegan, however, saw it otherwise. Influenced, perhaps, by factors overlooked by Dave and

8

possibly tired of the everlasting battle to survive in a hostile world, he had signed with Pride Seevert.

After that had come the quarrels, bitter and deep-scarring, in which Sam had reminded the boy that he was the father, Dave the son and as such he would make the decisions concerning the future of the Lazy K. It was at the end of one of these heated conversations that Dave had climbed onto his horse and ridden off.

He had never seen his father again, nor heard from him until a letter, written by Hannah Bradford, daughter of a neighboring rancher, had caught up with him on the Mexico–New Mexico border where he was working. Hannah had informed him of his father's death. She further stated that the Lazy K was steadily going to ruin, that he should return as soon as possible and take over. Fed up with drifting, Dave had replied at once, telling Hannah he was leaving within the week and giving her the approximate date of his arrival in Cabezon.

The engine topped the rise, started down the grade for the depot. *Almost there.* Keegan stared through the streaky glass of the window, wondered what to expect. Did Pride Seevert, along with his brothers Gabe and Chancy, still rule the Flats? Were they still

9

imposing their "combine" on the ranchers?

And what of the Lazy K? Hannah Bradford's letter had been two months running him down — had been written four months after the death of his father. Six months was a long time for a ranch to go untended.

Regardless, it was his and if it had fallen into ruin, as Hannah's note indicated, he'd simply have to start and rebuild. Rebuild? With what? He had something less than fifty dollars to his name, and he'd sold his horse and gear to raise that; but he'd make out. The Lazy K couldn't have decayed completely, and for cash he'd sell off a few head of beef.

As to the Seeverts — his ideas concerning them hadn't changed; he'd run his ranch to suit himself, and if it meant trouble he reckoned he could handle it. He was no fifteen year old boy now.

He watched the building that served as a depot rush forward to meet the train. It still needed paint, he saw, probably would continue to for another ten years while the cracks in the boards widened gradually and the yellow color faded steadily to an eventual dead white.

The stationmaster waited patiently on the built-up platform, and beyond him half a dozen loafers squatted in the shade. Farther along, near the hitchrack, three riders slouched on their saddles, eyeing the approaching engine expectantly.

Dave Keegan's jaw tightened. The one in the center astride a tall white horse was Chancy Seevert, the youngest brother — the one Dave had gone to school with. Chancy was waiting for him, he realized; waiting to talk, to find out where he stood, what his intentions were.

Keegan sighed quietly, settled back on the seat as the brakes of the coach clashed, began to screech. Absently, he reached for the pistol strapped to his hip, examined it briefly, allowed it to drop again into its oiled holster.

Welcome home — to trouble, he thought bitterly.

II

The train jolted to a halt. Dave Keegan got to his feet, walked the length of the car and stepped out into the bright sunlight. He nodded to the stationmaster, glanced curiously at the loafers, some of whom looked vaguely familiar, and then swung his attention to the men on horses, now moving up to the platform.

Chancy had changed considerably. He had filled out, was thicker through the chest, and his shoulders had widened. He had a cigar stuck in a corner of his mouth and as he spoke it bobbed up and down. Whatever it was that he said apparently was intended to be humorous, for the two punchers with him laughed dutifully.

They halted at the edge of the platform. Chancy brushed back his hat and grinned broadly.

"Howdy, stranger. Heard you was comin' back. We figured you ought to have a welcomin' committee."

Keegan moved his head slightly. He hadn't

given it any thought but he guessed now he should have written his reply to Hannah Bradford in a sealed envelope rather than on a postal card. Likely everyone on the Flats knew he was returning.

Chancy shifted the cigar to the opposite side of his mouth. "Just wanted you to know the deal we had with your pa'll still stand for you. Be nothin' changed."

So the Seeverts were still at it. Dave Keegan shook his head slowly. "No. The deal died with him. I'll handle my own stock."

Chancy Seevert's eyes narrowed. He ceased chewing on his weed. "Maybe," he murmured and looked around. Then, "What's wrong with the setup? Everybody else in the country's agreeable."

"Only because they don't want to fight you," Dave replied evenly, and paused. Behind him the train had begun to creak and groan as it again got under way.

"And you aim to," Seevert said when the racket had dwindled.

"If need be. I'm not paying the Seeverts or anybody else ten percent of my herd to market it — and standing trail losses and expenses, too. Cheaper to handle it myself."

Chancy shrugged. "There's been them who figured the same way, only they found out it was more expensive. A lot more."

13

One of the riders with Seevert laughed. Several of the loafers had risen and eased in nearer as if to hear better. The station agent lounged in the doorway of the depot, his expression intent.

"Be my problem," Keegan said coolly.

"And a powerful big one. What's the use of bein' mule-headed about it? Ain't nobody big enough to buck Seven Diamond."

"Don't intend to. If there's any trouble it'll come from your outfit."

Seevert sighed audibly. "Seems you had your mind made up before you ever got here," he said dryly. "I — "

"Made up my mind ten years ago," Dave cut in. "Nothing's changed it — nothing will."

Chancy flung away his cigar. "Reckon we'll just see about that," he said, and swung off the saddle.

Keegan waited quietly. Knowing Chancy Seevert he figured the second he stepped off the train that this moment had to come; Chancy always was one to settle things with his fists.

On the platform Seevert paused, unbuckled his gun belt and let it fall. He waited until Dave had followed suit.

"Be a right good time to change your mind," he said.

"Not now — not ever," Dave said, and taking three swift steps, drove his balled fist into Seevert's jaw.

Chancy yelled, staggered back and sat down. One of the onlookers shouted and the two Seven Diamond punchers started to climb off their horses, both scowling. Seevert waved them away and scrambled to his feet.

"I ain't needin' no help!" he rasped, and lunged at Keegan.

Dave leaped aside, smashed a blow into Chancy's ribs as he stumbled by. The momentum of it drove Seevert to his knees but he was up instantly and wheeling. Curses rumbled from his lips and a wild light filled his eyes.

"You goddam saddlebum — " he raged as he surged in. "I'll break you into pieces!"

"Got to hit him first!" someone in the crowd yelled.

Chancy seemed not to hear. Bent low he moved toward Dave, thick arms poised. Abruptly Keegan rushed. His churning fists met Seevert head on. There were half a dozen dry slapping sounds as they made contact. Chancy stalled, fell back. Dave bore in relentlessly, arms working like pistons. Seevert went to his knees.

From the corner of an eye Keegan saw the two punchers coming onto the platform.

15

He pulled back, prepared to meet attack from that quarter.

"Now, you boys just hold on," a dry, cracked voice sounded above the gusty breathing of Chancy Seevert. "Reckon this here shindig's between them two. Let's keep it that way."

Dave cast a glance over his shoulder. It was one of the loafers — a tall, hawk-faced old man who looked familiar. Weems . . . Pete Weems. . . . Recognition came to Dave in a flash. Weems owned, or had owned, a ranch to the west of the Lazy K. He had stepped in when the two Seven Diamond men had made their move, snatched up Keegan's pistol, was now pointing it carelessly in the direction of the pair. Keegan gave the old rancher a tight grin, brought his attention back to Seevert.

Chancy was upright but his eyes no longer held a brightness. His mouth hung open. He shook his head, shuffled forward. Dave eyed the man narrowly. Seevert was cunning; he appeared to be out on his feet but it could be a trick. Keegan retreated a step, another, keeping his guard up. Suddenly Chancy yelled and lunged. Dave, half expecting it, was still taken unexpectedly.

Pain flared through him as Seevert landed two solid blows to his head, followed with a third to the belly. One of the punchers shouted his encouragement. Chancy pressed his advantage, nailed Dave cleanly with another sharp blow to the ear. Keegan went to one knee, fighting to throw off the haze that was closing in.

He got back to his feet, lashed out blindly. His arm blocked the roundhouse swing Seevert had loosed and gave him another moment's respite. He moved off, back-pedaling slowly while his mind cleared. Suddenly Chancy was before him again, head low, crushed, bleeding lips split into a grin.

Keegan feinted, spun and came in fast from the side. Seevert, off balance, tried to wheel. Dave caught him with a left to the belly, a right that crackled when it connected with the man's jaw. Chancy yelled, threw himself forward, and caught Keegan around the waist.

Locked together they began to wrestle about on the platform, Dave hammering at Chancy's head and shoulders with his free hand while the squat rider struggled to tighten his grip around Keegan's waist. And then suddenly they were on the edge and going over.

Chancy was on the bottom, so took the brunt of the three foot drop. The throttling hand around Dave loosened. He wrenched free and bounded to his feet, dragging deep for wind. Seevert was up almost as quickly, that fixed grin still on his face. He rushed in, anxious to finish the fight.

Keegan set himself squarely, brought a right from his heels. The blow met Chancy straight on, popped like a whip when it landed. Seevert halted in his tracks. His arms fell. He stared at Dave through wide, glazed eyes and then dropped heavily into the dust.

Cheers went up from the platform. Dave stepped back, still heaving for breath. A hand clapped him on the shoulder and Pete Weems's voice shouted in his ear.

"Boy — you done done it! Town's been waitin' years to see this!"

Keegan nodded woodenly. His body ached and there were places on his face where Chancy's knuckles had removed the skin and set up a sharp stinging. After a moment he turned away. Weems dropped off the platform, thrust his belt and gun into his hands.

"Expect you ought to be strappin' this on, Dave," the old puncher said. He paused, lifted his brows. "You are Sam Keegan's boy, ain't you?"

Dave nodded, buckled on his weapon.

"Figured as much from what was bein' said. You're back to take over your pa's place, I'm guessin'."

Again Keegan nodded. "That's what this was all about."

"Way I understood it. Just wanted to be sure."

The two Seven Diamond punchers moved up, looked questioningly at Dave and then at Chancy, still flat on the ground. Keegan nodded curtly, reached back onto the platform and retrieved his hat.

"You'll be needin' some help. I'm askin' for a job right now."

Dave frowned, glanced at the older man. "What about your own place?"

"Ain't mine no more," Weems said, his lips pulling tight. "Got euchred outta it by the Seeverts — same as a lot of other folks did. Am I hired?"

"We'll talk about it later," Keegan replied. "Right now I need a drink — bad."

The two punchers had Chancy on his feet, but he was still out. The taller of the pair paused, faced Dave.

"You're goin' to be needin' more'n a drink, once he comes to," he said in a promising voice.

Dave shrugged, pointed to the Fan-Tan saloon down the street.

"That's where he'll find me," he said and, trailed by Pete Weems, moved off through the ankle-deep dust.

III

Simmering, Dave Keegan allowed his glance to swing from side to side as he strode toward the saloon. Weems said something but he did not hear; he was seeing the town just as it had been ten years ago. The Gem Cafe . . . Cabezon Bank & Trust Co . . . Dollarhide's Hotel . . . Herman's Livery Stable . . . R. Raskob, Gen'l. Mchdse. . . . Miss Pringle's Ladies Shop. . . . Nothing had changed.

Cabezon had stagnated under the rule of Pride Seevert and his brothers — and those who lived there were aware of such. But they would do nothing about it just as surely as they would resent his return, for they knew he would never accept the Seven Diamond yoke, and that meant trouble. But it would be his problem, not theirs, and he would keep it so.

They reached the Fan-Tan and turned into the open doorway. The place was cool, shadowy and almost deserted. Dave crossed to a table in the back corner, sat down facing the street and signaled to the bartender for a bottle and glasses. Pete Weems, mopping at the sweat on his beet-red cheeks, dropped into the chair at Keegan's left.

"From the looks some of them folks was givin' us, I'd reckon you ain't goin' to be real popular here on the Flats."

"Had the feeling myself," Dave replied, filling the glasses. After a moment he added, "Guess I expected it."

The old rancher downed his liquor in a single gulp and blinked. "You right sure it's worth it — takin' on the Seeverts, I mean?"

"I didn't come here just to fight Pride and the others. I came back to run my ranch."

Weems nodded slowly. "The two go together — unless you do it Pride's way."

Dave started to speak, then paused, eyes on the street. The two Seven Diamond riders, with Chancy Seevert between them, were passing in front of the doorway. None of the three glanced toward the saloon; they simply continued on down the street.

Pete Weems grinned, rubbed at the stubble on his chin, " 'Pears Chancy's had enough for one day."

Keegan smiled briefly, sipped at his drink. "You see much of my pa before he died?"

"Two, maybe three times a year. Mostly while I still had my place. Toward the last he just sort of give up, let Pride and his bunch do what they like." Weems hesitated, then added, "You ain't goin' to find much left of the ranch, son. Went to hell mighty fast."

"The Seeverts?"

"Well, maybe partly. Sam just sort of quit, like I said. Didn't take no interest in anythin'."

"Any stock left?"

"Not that I know of. You'll have to build up a herd from scratch."

"Be hard to do unless I can get the bank to go along with me."

Weems wagged his head. "Don't go pinnin' much hope on Tom Gower. He's Pride's man."

"Who isn't?" Dave said with a short laugh.

The rancher looked down at his glass, began to twirl it between his fingers. "Me — for one. And Herman Gooch at the livery stable. Maybe a couple more."

"Cass Bradford — where does he stand? Was his little girl who wrote me about Pa."

"With the others. Ain't much else a man can do unless he's honin' for a right smart of trouble. Man has to think about his family, but I always had a feelin' Cass'd kick over the traces was ever he to get a chance."

Pete checked his words, cocked his head to one side. "And that little girl you're talking about — she ain't no girl no longer, she's quite a woman. You forgettin' she's growed some in ten years?"

He had, Dave realized with a start. Hannah Bradford would be twenty or so — and he was still picturing her in his mind as a spindly little kid with pigtails and freckles across her nose.

"Pretty as a moonflower, too," Weems went on. "Got most of the young bucks around here gettin' their hair cut regular-like. Even Chancy Seevert."

"He have any luck?"

"Not with her. She's a spunky one. He tried shining up to her for a spell, finally give up." Pete chuckled. "One time the See-vert name didn't mean nothin'. You say it was her that wrote you?"

Dave nodded, refilled the glasses. "Reckon I'd better drop by and pay my respects, first chance I get. Anybody new on the Flats?"

"Folks don't ever move in here — they move out. Little man ain't got a chance under Seevert's deal. Goes broke quick."

"That what happened to you?"

"Along with the hard winter we had in seventy-eight. Never did have much of a herd, as you'll recollect, and what with payin' the Seeverts ten percent and what I lost in the freeze, I was down to nothin'. I'd a made it, howsomever, if it hadn't been for that ten percent."

"You just walk off?"

"Sold out to Pride. Was real generous to me. Give me about ten cents on the dollar for my holdin's. Knew I was in a squeeze with the bank breathin' down my neck, and that I'd take whatever he offered. Always will believe he went to Tom Gower and found out how much I owed, then made that his price."

That would be the way Pride Seevert would handle it, Dave thought. There had been a time, when old Horace Seevert was alive, that Seven Diamond stood for honesty and fairness. All changed when Pride, eldest of the three sons, took over.

The freshly turned earth was scarcely dry on his father's grave when he'd called a meeting of all ranchers on the Flats and served up what amounted to little less than an ultimatum. Matters had not been the same since, and Pride, using his brothers Gabe and Chancy as iron-fisted persuaders, was still riding high.

Dave stared with unseeing eyes through the doorway. What chance did he have against the Seeverts? Broke, inheritor of a neglected, run-down ranch, and with the hand of almost every one on the Flats turned against him

— how could he hope to survive? He didn't know the answer to that but he knew he must — somehow.

A man had a right to what was his, along with the privilege of living his life as he saw fit — and that all added up to running the Lazy K according to his own ideas. And that's what he intended to do, or at least, attempt to do. If he didn't at least try he knew he'd never be able to live with himself.

"About that there job — "

Dave roused at the gentle prodding of Pete Weems.

"You never give me no answer. Am I hired?"

"You are," Keegan said, pushing back his chair. "We're going to work right now."

The old puncher grinned broadly. "Sounds mighty good to me. What's first off?"

Dave rose, dug into his pocket for a coin to pay for the drinks and dropped it on the table.

"Have a talk with Gower at the bank, see if I've got any credit there."

"Can give you the answer to that right now," Weems said morosely. "Tom ain't doin' nothin' that'll cross him up with the Seeverts."

"Want him to tell me that," Keegan said,

starting for the door. "If that's the how of it, then we'll figure something else. One way or another we're putting the Lazy K back on its feet."

IV

Tom Gower was sitting at his huge rolltop desk when they entered the bank. He was alone except for the teller behind his wire cage, and the expression on his lean features was guarded as he looked up.

"How are you, Keegan?"

"Good," Dave replied, and came right to the point. "You interested in my business?"

Gower toyed with a paper-cluttered spindle. "Be glad to have your account, of course. You want to make a deposit now?"

"Not what I had in mind. Was thinking of a loan. Intend to start working my ranch — will be needing a little cash to buy cattle with."

Gower shook his head slowly. "Times are a bit hard — "

"I'm willing to put up the property and the cattle as security. Not much of a risk for you."

"Realize that — but money's tight. I'm having to watch our loans — "

Anger pushed through Dave Keegan. He

27

took a half step forward. "Why don't you lay it on the line? What you mean is that Pride Seevert wouldn't like it!"

The banker's face darkened. "I run this place," he said stiffly. "I decide who — "

"You decide — as long as it's all right with him!"

"Not the way of it — "

"Forget it! Don't even bother to talk it over with him. I'll make other arrangements."

Dave spun about, shouldering up against Pete Weems, who had been standing behind him, and came to a full stop. The squat figure of Dewey Dalton, owner of one of the larger ranches on the Flats, came through the doorway. Dalton halted, staring at Dave.

"Keegan!" he said in a surprised voice. "Heard you were coming back — hoped it wasn't so. You ain't changed much in looks — how about otherwise?"

Again anger burned through Dave. "If you mean Pride Seevert, there's no change there either."

"You aim to take over your pa's place, start ranchin'?"

"It's my place now," Keegan said quietly, "and I intend to rebuild it and run it my way."

Dalton's eyes squinted. "And to hell with everybody else, that it? Country's a powder

28

keg now, just waiting for somebody to strike a spark. That could be you."

"Then the smart thing for you to do is pass the word to the Seeverts to leave me alone."

"Which they won't — you know damned well!" Dalton shouted. "All right! When Pride starts clamping down, don't come running to the rest of us for help! Maybe we don't exactly like the way things go but we've got sense enough to ride along when we've got no other choice."

Keegan shifted his shoulders. "Just another way of admitting Pride Seevert's got you by the throat and you don't have guts enough to shake him off."

Pete Weems laughed softly. Dalton flushed. "We're doing all right," he murmured defensively. "Making a little money, and having no trouble. Smarten up, Keegan. String along with the rest of us. Things'll change."

"Seems they haven't in the last ten years. Way it looks, they won't in the next ten."

"And you figure you can do something about that."

"Not even going to try, far as you and the rest are concerned. I'm just aiming to run the Lazy K to suit myself."

Abruptly, Dave moved forward, pushed by Dalton and returned to the street. Pete Weems was chuckling at his shoulder.

"You sure hit old Dewey where it hurt," he said, and then suddenly he was sober. "You got yourself an idea now how the rest of the ranchers'll be feelin' about it. They just plain won't want you around. You're pickin' a hard row to hoe."

Dave grinned at the old puncher. "If you think that, why're you so anxious to line up with me?"

Weems scratched at his chin, laughed. "Well, now, I ain't right sure, but I reckon I seen Pride Seevert's comeuppance standin' there on the depot platform beatin' the hell out of Chancy and figured I wanted to be in on it!"

"Pride's not going to think it's funny. And he plays for keeps."

"So what? I ain't ascared of bullets. Way I feel I could die happy was I to see him crawlin' around, eatin' dirt. . . . What's next?"

"Raskob. We'll be needing supplies."

Weems spat. "Wastin' your time again. You'll get the same runaround Tom Gower handed you."

"There another general store in town?"

"Nope."

"Then we'll have to try Raskob," Dave said and stepped off the boardwalk into the street.

They crossed, mounted the two steps to

the porch and entered the low-roofed building. The thin, spare figure of the merchant, wearing an apron and a green eye-shade, emerged from a room off the back, halted. Keegan, trailed by Weems, threaded his way through the piles of harness, tables of housewares, and racks of clothing, and pulled up at the counter. Raskob greeted him warily.

"You want my trade?" Dave asked bluntly.

The merchant's eyes flickered briefly, and then he shrugged. "You know the situation around here. Ought to answer that for you."

"In other words if I'm a friend of the Seeverts, you're interested."

"But you're not. I seen that little fracas down at the depot. No use claiming — "

"Don't intend to. Point is — you willing to sell me what I need or not? Say it — straight out."

"I — I can't, Keegan. You've got to see my — "

"All I wanted to know," Dave said, and holding tight to his temper, wheeled and moved back through the clutter of merchandise to the street.

Almost immediately a voice from down the way hailed him. "Dave Keegan — it iss you, eh? Sam's boy, eh?"

"It's Dutch — Herman Gooch," Weems said.

Dave nodded. He remembered the livery stable owner. He lifted his hand in salutation, headed for the sprawling structure.

Gooch, a ponderous man with a moon-like face, gave him a firm handclasp, slapped him on the shoulder. "It iss good you have come back. . . . A man you are now."

"Good to see you again," Dave said.

The stableman sank back into his chair, leaned against the wall. "You move onto the old place, yes?"

"What I figure to do. Outside of Pete here I'm not getting much encouragement, however. Seems I'm plenty unpopular. Talking to me's not going to do you any good, Dutch."

Gooch's round face sobered. He wagged his head dolefully. "It iss sad. I come to this country because it has no kings, no barons who can say if you live or die. America iss a free land, I tell myself. There I should be. Now it iss here. It follows me. It should not be so."

"Outside of Pete, you're the only one feeling that way."

Gooch shifted his massive bulk. "They are fools! They do not understand what it iss to be a free man. Slavery they do not believe in yet they give it roots to grow. It iss like a disease — will grow — spread, and soon it cannot be stopped. I tell them this — Gower, Dollarhide, Raskob, but they will not believe."

"Ain't the only ones," Pete Weems said. "Dutch, Dave's needin' help to get started on his pa's place. You reckon you could do him any good?"

"What I can do, I will! You only ask, boy."

Keegan shook his head. Herman Gooch was a businessman and he could suffer for his actions.

"Don't want to get you in trouble with the Seeverts and some of the others around."

Gooch shook a fat finger at him. "You leave the Seeverts to me. And the others. Before you were born I learn to deal with their kind in the old country. What will you need?"

Keegan studied the man, smiled. "You're not afraid of getting hurt?"

"I am too old for fear. And always there iss a way to skin cats, even the mean ones. What do you want?"

"Horses and tack for Pete and me — for one thing. Don't know for certain what's left at the ranch. Have to take a look, make out a list."

"Grub," Weems said.

Herman Gooch bobbed his head. "It iss

33

easy. Horses and tools I can give you from here. Grub I will buy from Raskob. He will sell to me even though he knows it iss for you."

"They're all scared, Dutch. Can't blame him too much."

"Such makes no difference! A man cannot be a rabbit! A man must fight for what iss right, or soon he will have no rights." Gooch paused, motioned to Weems. "Pete — the horses in the back corral. Pick what iss needed. Saddles and bridles you will find in the harness shed."

The old puncher nodded, moved off into the stable. Dave said, "I'll have to ask you for credit, Dutch. Soon as I get things going I'll pay you — "

"Pay! What iss pay? Sam was to me a kind friend. This much I owe him, and more."

"I've got a few dollars. I can take care of the stuff you get from Raskob."

"The few dollars you will keep for other things. Some day, when all goes well for you at your ranch, we will make a settlement."

"I don't like — "

"What iss it you don't like — that I would be a good friend to the son of my good friend Sam? There iss no need for more talk of it. All is arranged. Understood?"

"Understood," Dave said slowly. "And thanks. Means a lot to me."

Gooch waved off the expression of appreciation. "You ride to the ranch today?"

"Soon as we can saddle up."

"Good. Bring your list to me and all the rest I will do." The stableman thrust forth his hand. "Good luck, boy."

"Thanks again," Keegan replied. "Expect I'll be needing it."

V

Half an hour later Keegan was on the road leading west from Cabezon. He was alone. Pete Weems had decided to take that opportunity for dropping by the cabin where he had set up residence and picking up his belongings. He was to rejoin Dave later at the Lazy K.

The morning sun was at his back and it felt good to be in the saddle again, to have a horse under him. Weems had chosen a tough little buckskin gelding for him, one not much for looks but barrel-chested and sturdy and built for hard work. Mentally he again thanked Dutch Gooch for his help and hoped it would not lead to trouble for the stableman.

A short distance from the settlement the road forked, the trail to the left continuing westward, the other angling toward the towering crags of Tenkiller Mountain and the ranches that lay against it. Here, for a brief expanse, was a narrow strip of country commonly called the Roughs. Its rocky, sandy soil supported little other than snakeweed and small desert flowers that managed to grow despite adverse conditions.

Now, as in the past, Keegan hastened to cross this intervening slice of wasteland that separated the lower flats from the mountain lushness, and soon was loping into the more desirable area of trees and grass-covered ground. Things looked good. It must have been a fine spring, he thought, and hoped he would find the Lazy K range in equally excellent condition.

He reached Wolf River with its wild cherry and plum lined banks, forded the knee-deep stream while a hundred memories of the past — of the times he had swum in the icy water, hunted cottontails in the brush, picked fruit and berries — crowded into his mind. Those were the good days before the Seeverts had risen to heights of ruthless power; he wondered if such would ever change, if the Flats could ever be as they had been.

He followed the banks of the river, keeping to a well-marked trail running close to the water's edge, and thus avoided the road. He had no particular reasons for taking such measures other than it was cool and pleasant along the Wolf and it made him think of the days when he was growing up.

The slopes of Tenkiller began to take substance as he drew nearer, and he could make out the long canyons filled with brush and rock, the higher ledges and hogbacks that linked the peaks. Far to the right he could see the Flats proper, looking like a gray-green sea with their coverlet of grass.

He came to the point where the river entered the eastern boundary of Dewey Dalton's spread and he paused there. He was in no mood to encounter the squat, hard-talking rancher again, and considered the advisability of swinging away from the stream. But Dalton likely was still in Cabezon and after a few moments Keegan rode on, keeping to the banks of the Wolf.

He crossed Double-D range without interruption and shortly was riding into Box C territory, owned by Ed Corrigan — or at least it had been Corrigan's ten years ago. Almost immediately he saw two horsemen break out of timber half a mile to his left and lope toward him. Dave pushed on, having no reason to fear interception; Ed Corrigan had been a friend of his father's and there was no cause to be disturbed.

He watched the two men halt, wait for him at a bend in the trail. One was a stranger of about his own age; the other, much older, he recognized from the past. The younger man rode forward to meet him, his face hard and set under his broad-brimmed hat.

"Mister, you know where you are?" he demanded.

Keegan pulled the buckskin to a stop, smiled amiably. "Reckon I do."

"This here's Box C range. Didn't you see the markers when you come to them?"

Dave looked beyond the puncher to his companion. The older man was studying him thoughtfully.

"I saw them," Keegan said. "Fact is, I helped put them there."

"Well, Mr. Corrigan don't care much for drifters traipsin' across his land, so I — " the rider said and then caught at his words. He frowned, started to say more but the older man spoke first.

"Say — you wouldn't be Sam Keegan's boy . . . ?"

Dave grinned. "I would. And you're Asa Bowersox . . . I remember you now."

The old rider's mouth broke into a crooked smile. He kneed his horse forward, shook Dave's hand.

"Right glad to see you again. What're you doin' around here — passin' through?"

Keegan glanced at the young puncher, scowling in quiet suspicion. Bowersox nodded.

"That's Billy Joe Hinkle — we call him

Primo. Primo, meet Dave Keegan. His pa's place's over there t'other side of the short hills."

Hinkle took Dave's hand soberly. His eyes had brightened with narrow interest, but he said nothing.

"You just ridin' through?" Asa asked once more.

"No, figure to start up the Lazy K, get it going again."

Bowersox looked down. "Fear you won't find much left."

"Been hearing that. Doesn't matter. Land's still there, and that's what counts."

"Mr. Corrigan know about this?" Billy Joe asked suddenly.

Temper moved through Keegan. He faced the puncher. "Some reason he should?"

Asa Bowersox bridged the abrupt quiet. "Primo don't mean nothin'. Just takes his job real serious-like. Your ranch — reckon you can do what you want with it."

"Intend to," Dave said bluntly. He shifted his attention to Bowersox. "If you're up my way, drop in. Be glad to see you."

"I'll do that," the old puncher said. "Adios."

"Adios," Keegan answered and rode on.

A short time later he reached the end of Box C range and entered his own range.

40

Following the trail across a flat meadow, he climbed a small rise, dropped again to level ground. There he halted, his eyes on the almost obscured road that he and his father, by dint of much sweat and back-breaking toil, had hacked through the brush.

The ruts had filled with grass but their course was still evident; the rocks they had rolled aside, the trees they had felled — all were still apparent. He studied it all briefly, having his moments of recollection, and then moved on, anxious now for a glimpse of the house itself.

He entered the clearing and pulled up. The building was before him — old and sagging, its windows gaping, empty eyes. The porch had collapsed at one end, the slanting roof providing a playground for two striped ground squirrels that scurried off at his appearance.

The well house had been toppled, and fire had all but consumed the shed where he had once stabled, in favored, solitary majesty, his first pony. The remaining outbuildings were graying shells, some upright, some canted drunkenly, others simply prone. The Lazy K had not died six months ago when Sam Keegan passed on; it appeared to have been dead for years.

Heavy with despair, Dave rode in closer,

halted at the remains of the hitchrack. It was worse than he had expected; he had spoken of rebuilding — there was little to rebuild from other than the land itself. But he could make out — he would. He'd begin —

The sudden, sharp crack of a rifle, the dull *thunk* of a bullet smashing into the wooden planks of the wall beyond him, scattered Dave Keegan's thoughts. Instinctively, he went off the saddle in a long dive, plunged through the open doorway into the house.

The rifle slapped again. Dust spurted at Keegan's heels. He dragged out his pistol, crawled to a window and peered over the sill. There was no one in sight. Cocking the forty-five, he waited for the next shot, hoping for a smoke puff that would allow him to target the marksman in ambush.

There was only the hot silence, and then, faintly, he heard the rapid tattoo of a horse beating a retreat eastward. Whoever had thrown the shots at him was pulling out.

Dave rose slowly, slid his pistol back into its holster. The meaning of the incident was clear; the rifleman had not meant to hit him — only to warn. In strong language he had been told to forget the Lazy K, to move on.

Grim-faced, Keegan moved back into the open. It would have been one of Pride

Seevert's men looking down that rifle barrel at him. Or would it? Seevert, ordinarily, was not the kind to serve warnings. Then who? He shook off the question angrily. It didn't matter. Nobody was going to drive him off his ranch.

VI

He began work at once. The rails of the corral were down and after picketing the buckskin nearby he rummaged around until he located a few tools and with those he set to putting the kitchen and one room of the house in passable order. Such would afford temporary shelter for him and Pete Weems; later, when funds and time permitted, he would build a new house.

He had just finished with the second of the slat bunks when Weems rode into the yard and dismounted. The old puncher looked around slowly, shook his head.

"Sure in bad shape. Worse'n I figured."

"It'll do," Dave replied. "We'll have a place to sleep and a stove to cook on. Improvements'll come later." He reached into his shirt pocket, drew forth a slip of paper. "Here's the list for Gooch. Been making it as I went along."

Pete studied the items, whistled softly. "Powerful lot of stuff."

Keegan nodded. "We won't have time to

go running into town every few days. Expect that to hold us for a month or so."

"Sure ought to. You want me to take it to Dutch now?"

"Hate to ask you to make that ride again but I guess you'll have to. We'll be needing grub for supper tonight."

"Don't mind," Weems said, tossing his bundle of spare clothing onto one of the bunks. " 'Spect I can make it back by dark."

Dave said, "Be fine." He pointed at the pistol on the puncher's hip. "Keep that handy. Had me a visitor right after I got here."

Weems frowned. "Somebody shootin' at you?"

"Twice. From the brush."

"You get a look at whoever it was?"

"No. He pulled out without showing himself."

Weems swore deeply. "The Seeverts. Had to be them."

"Maybe. Could've been somebody from town — or one of the ranchers wanting me to keep moving so's I wouldn't stir up any trouble. Doesn't matter."

"Not scarin' you off any, eh?"

"Take more'n that."

Pete grinned. "Good. They want a scrap, we'll give it to 'em," he said and turned for his horse. "Be a right smart idea for you to keep your eyes peeled, too."

"Aim to do that," Dave said, and watched the man ride out of the yard.

By the middle of the afternoon he had accomplished all he could until the supplies arrived, and needing a drink to quench his thirst, crossed to the well. He found the pulley broken and the bucket shot full of bullet holes, but a rock dropped into the shaft told him water was still available.

He walked then to a small spring a hundred yards or so below the yard, satisfied his needs, mentally noting that he and Weems would have to use that source until the well was put back in shape.

After that he visited the small hill where his mother was buried, found the townspeople had also placed his father there. He spent a little time replacing the rocks that had washed aside and cleaning up the weeds, then returned finally to the house to await Pete Weems's arrival. He hadn't noticed it earlier but he was beginning to feel hunger.

Shortly after dark he heard the thud of horses' hooves and the grate of iron tires cutting into the soil. He rose quickly from his bunk, and hand resting on the butt of his pistol, moved to the window where he could have a full view of the yard. A minute later Herman Gooch, driving a spring wagon, with Weems on the seat beside him, came into view. Keegan relaxed, stepped out into the yard.

The livery stableman drew to a stop in front of the door. Pete stood up.

"Was so much stuff Dutch figured he'd better haul it in a wagon," he explained, climbing down.

Gooch smiled widely. "Also, I want to see your place. I have not been this far from town in many years. A man gets old and fat." He paused, glanced around. "It iss a big job you have here."

Dave shrugged. "You run into any trouble?"

Gooch said, "No — no trouble. With Raskob business iss business so long as his nose is kept clean."

Pete, already beginning to unload, said, "I didn't see nobody neither."

Keegan moved up to help the old puncher. Gooch crawled off the wagon, grunting and groaning at the effort. Sitting down on the edge of the porch, he mopped at his face.

"Weems has told me of the shooting. He did not come again?"

"Just that one time. Guess they're giving me time to think it over."

"But you do not change, eh? Good . . . good."

47

He watched in silence after that while the two men transferred the load of supplies into the house and alongside, and then rose to take his leave. Keegan waved him back.

"Stay for a bite of supper. Won't be much but it'll keep you going until you can get to town."

Gooch agreed readily and all moved into the kitchen. Together Dave and Pete Weems prepared a meal of fried potatoes, meat, cornbread and coffee. For dessert they opened a can of peaches. Finished, they went back into the coolness of the yard and using some of the wooden boxes the supplies had come in as chairs, they settled back for a smoke.

"Expect it was you who looked after Pa when he died," Dave said after a few moments had passed. "Want to thank you for it."

"Was several of us," the stableman said. "Bradford, Ed Corrigan, Pete — even Raskob. We put Sam next to his wife. We think he would want it so."

"Where he should be. I'll thank the others, too. If there was any expense — "

"There was nothing," Dutch cut in. He stared at the glowing coal in his curved stem pipe. "You have made a start here. Now what will you do for cattle?"

"Thought I'd talk to Cass Bradford, see

if he'd sell me enough to start a herd. Always was friendly enough."

Gooch nodded slowly. "Bradford iss a fine man, but help you I am not sure. He iss obligated to the bank — to Tom Gower. And Gower . . ."

"He's under Pride Seevert's thumb," Pete Weems completed. "Reckon Cass'd like to help but he won't take no chances."

"Means I'll take a ride to Junction City then, have a talk with the banker up there. Figure this place ought to be good enough for a small loan."

Keegan looked questioningly at the stableman, seeking verification. Gooch bobbed his head.

"It iss so — and if recommendation by me iss needed, I will give it. You tell the banker."

"Be obliged," Keegan said. "But already you have done too much."

"Too much!" Gooch echoed, pulling himself laboriously to his feet. "It iss very little compared to what you have in mind to do. . . . Now I must go."

Dave and Weems followed the man to his wagon, aided him to the seat. When he had settled his ponderous bulk, he took up the reins and looked down at Keegan.

"There will be things you forgot. Send

for them. And for the meal, you have my thanks."

"You have mine," Keegan said as Gooch wheeled the vehicle about and cut back to the road. "So long."

"So long," the stable owner called back, waving his thick hand.

Keegan and Weems returned to the kitchen, untouched after the meal. Pete began to stack the tin plates.

"Let it go till morning," Dave said, reaching for the lantern. "We both need a night's sleep."

Weems signified his agreement, followed Dave into the room where bunks had been constructed. "Was just thinkin', we're goin' to be right busy, you and me. Be a good idea was we to get us a cook."

Keegan kicked off his boots, lay back on his blankets. "Have to raise some money before we can do much of anything — much less hire help."

"Feller I'm thinkin' about won't need no wages. Be glad to work for found and keep."

"Kind of hands we're needing," Keegan muttered. "We'll talk about it in the morning."

His eyes were heavy and his muscles ached from the unaccustomed labor. He was too beat to even undress. Vaguely, he heard

Weems stirring about and then it was dark as the lantern was turned down. Pete said something but Dave only half heard.

In the next moment he was sitting on the edge of the bunk. Daylight brightened the room and he realized what had seemed but short minutes actually were hours during which he had slept soundly. Weems, snoring gently, had not awakened.

Dave frowned. What had roused him? A noise — a sound of some sort? Tension suddenly building within him, he slipped quietly from the bunk and made his way to the window in the next room. Keeping well back he peered through the glassless opening.

Chancy Seevert, flanked by half a dozen Seven Diamond riders, was pulling to a halt in the yard.

VII

Dave wheeled instantly, silently, returned to his bunk. Pulling on his boots and strapping on his gun, he shook Weems roughly. The old puncher rolled over.

"On your feet!" Keegan said in a hoarse whisper.

Pete sat up, rubbed at his jaw. "What's wrong?"

"Chancy — and a bunch of his hard-cases. Out front."

Weems was on his feet instantly, pulling on his clothing. From the yard Seevert's harsh voice issued a summons.

"Keegan — come out here!"

"Probably figure I'm alone," Dave said hurriedly. "Take your rifle — go out the back — but don't let them see you. I'll signal if I need help."

"Keegan! You hear me?"

Dave turned, crossed the room and stepped lazily into the open. A hard grin cracked Chancy Seevert's lips.

"Well, now — here's our squatter, boys.

Reckon we got him outta bed."

The rider beside him laughed. "Looks like he's gone and fixed hisself a reg'lar roost in that there shack."

"And all for nothin'," another said.

Keegan leaned against the wall of the house. Folding his arms he studied Seevert coldly. "What's on your mind?"

"You," Chancy replied bluntly. "Ain't very smart, comin' out here. Thought I made that plain yesterday."

"Other way around. Was me made it clear I intended to do what I want. One look at you proves it."

Chancy's swollen and skinned face darkened. He shifted his weight, glared angrily.

"And taking potshots at me's not going to work either."

Seevert frowned. "What's that mean?"

"That bushwhacker you sent out here yesterday to scare me off — "

"You're loco . . . I never sent nobody."

Chancy was genuinely surprised. Evidently it had been someone from town, or perhaps a rancher hoping to head off trouble.

"Doesn't matter. Point is you and your friends might as well get it straight — I'm here to stay."

"You are like hell! You ain't stayin' unless you line up with the rest of the Flats. We're

53

runnin' things around here, Keegan!"

Dave smiled quietly. "Not me — not the Lazy K, you're not," he said, deliberately baiting the man.

Seevert's eyes narrowed as his flush mounted. "You're sure askin' for it, mister. I rode over here this mornin', friendly-like, to give you another chance. But if you think I'm goin' to let you smart-mouth me — "

"I'm just telling you what's what. I'm having nothing to do with the Seeverts."

"We'll see about that!" Chancy yelled and piled off his horse. "When I get through with you, you'll be wishin' you'd never even heard of this country. Couple of you boys — grab him, hold him for me!"

Dave stepped quickly off the porch into the yard as the riders next to Chancy dropped to the ground, began to move in.

"You ever try doing something without help?" Keegan asked acidly.

Chancy grinned. "Nice thing about bein' the top dog. Can do things the easy way."

"Could be you've got a little mush in your backbone, too," Keegan said, and then turning his head, called: "All right, Pete — let 'em know where you are."

The loud click of a Winchester being levered broke through the hush. The two men siding Chancy froze. Weems stepped from behind a clump of brush at the side of the house, rifle leveled.

"Reckon we'll keep this argument same as it was yesterday — just between them two," the old puncher said. "I'm servin' notice right now — first one of you that tries to take a hand gets a bullet in his belly."

Keegan beckoned to Seevert. "You were in a big hurry a minute ago. Come on — let's get on with it."

Chancy did not move. He glanced at Weems, then at the men behind him. He shook his head. "You ain't gettin' away with this!" he yelled suddenly. "You ain't pushin' me around — "

Keegan lunged forward, grabbed Seevert by the shirt front. Swinging him half about, he slapped the man smartly across the face.

"You goddam four-flusher — I do what I please on my own place!" he shouted, abruptly angry. "You tell that to Pride and Gabe — and anybody else that's interested!"

Shoving hard, he sent Seevert stumbling back to his horse.

"Now get on that saddle and pull out! I ever see you or any Seven Diamond man on my property again I'll start shooting. Hear?"

Chancy, off balance and clinging to his horse, managed to recover his feet. Without looking up he slid his foot into the stirrup and swung aboard. Face tipped down he wheeled about and started for the road. Silent, the others filed in behind him.

Pistol in hand, Dave watched them leave. He heard Pete Weems move up to stand beside him. The old puncher was chuckling in a low, throaty rumble. But there was no humor in the moment for Keegan. All the bars were down now and the matter was far from being finished.

"Made him eat dirt — that you sure did," Weems murmured. "Was a sight for sore eyes!"

Chancy and his men had halted at the edge of the yard. Dave, alert, took a step forward, gun half lifted. Seevert stared, shook his head, and rode on.

"They've always been the ones to play rough," Pete continued. "Now, buckin' up against somebody that hands it right back sure has stopped old Chancy cold. He jus' don't know how to figure it!"

Dave Keegan's attention was still on the brush beyond which the Seven Diamond men had disappeared. After a moment he heard the steady drum of running horses, knew they had gone on. Only then did he holster his weapon.

"Let's get something to eat," he said, turning for the door. "Then I'm taking a run over to Bradford about some stock. Got a chore for you while I'm gone."

Weems let off the hammer of his rifle. "What's that?"

"Want you to string a wire through the brush around the yard, knee high or so. Then hang some tin cans on it. Anybody tries sneaking in on us, we'll know it."

"Mostly Chancy — I take it."

"Chancy — and maybe whoever it was that took those shots at me yesterday."

VIII

An hour later Dave Keegan was on the buckskin and moving north through the fetlock-deep grass of his upper range. His final words to Pete Weems had been to keep an eye open for trouble and not to attempt a defense should the Seeverts return; if they came they'd come in numbers and one man would have no chance against them.

"Reckon you're the one that'd better do some watchin'," the old puncher had countered. "Chancy ain't goin' to draw a long breath till he's squared up for what you done to him this mornin'."

There was no doubt in the truth of that statement, "I'll keep a sharp lookout," he had assured Pete. "You do the same."

Keegan felt it was unlikely, however, that they would see any more of Seven Diamond that day. There would be repercussions. He wasn't fooling himself on that — he had been fully aware of the possibilities when he roughed up Chancy. But it would be the Seeverts' way to bide their time, wait for

58

the moment when they could move in unexpectedly and catch the opposition off guard.

The bushwhacker was something else. Whoever he was, he could try again — and perhaps this time not purposely miss with his shots.

Aware of this possibility, Dave took closer note of the country through which he was passing but when he finally reached the rise from which he could look down on Cass Bradford's Quarter-Circle B spread he guessed that the mysterious marksman, too, was holding off.

He started down the long, gradual slope. Far below he could see the scatter of buildings and trees that made up the Bradford place. On beyond those Wolf River cut a silver slash through the green carpet, and to the south numerous dots on the hazy landscape marked the location of part of the herd.

Reaching level ground, he loped across a flinty meadow, entered the yard and pulled to a halt at the hitchrack. Bradford, apparently having heard Dave's approach, stepped out onto his porch, a smile on his lips.

"Light a spell," the rancher said. "Got coffee on the stove."

Keegan dismounted and moved up onto the long gallery that fronted the house, took the rancher's extended hand. His clasp was firm and his greeting cordial. Dave felt his hopes rise.

"Can't see as you've changed much," Bradford said, motioning to one of the several chairs. "Bigger, filled out." He looked toward the door. "Hannah — how about that coffee?"

Dave made himself comfortable in a cowhide rocker. "Seems nothing much has changed on the Flats, either."

Cass Bradford gave him a keen look. "Meaning Pride Seevert?"

Keegan nodded. He started to say more when the door opened and Hannah appeared with a tray on which were cups, sugar and cream, and a pot of coffee. Dave got to his feet. Pete Weems had not done Hannah justice; she was a beautiful girl.

"Hello, Dave," she said, placing the tray on a table. "It's good to see you again."

"Good to be back," he mumbled, and then finding himself, added, "Want to say I'm obliged to you — again — for writing me about Pa."

"Thought you ought to know," Hannah said. "Have you moved back onto your place yet?"

Dave nodded. "Yesterday. Got Pete Weems working for me. Ranch's run down plenty bad."

Cass Bradford leaned forward. "Pride Seevert know that — that you're back on your place, I mean?"

Temper lifted within Keegan. "Expect he does. Had Chancy waiting at the depot for me yesterday morning," he said stiffly. "Paid me another call a few hours ago."

The rancher's face was sober. "I take it you've not changed your mind about Pride's deal."

"Not a bit."

Bradford shook his head, settled back with a sigh. "Hate to think of all hell breaking loose around here again."

"It won't, long as they leave me alone."

"Pride's in no position to do that. He lets you get away with it, then there'll be others. It'll be like a dam: if you don't repair the first crack, the whole works goes."

"Be the best thing that could happen to this country," Dave said. "You can't deny that."

"Maybe, but a man pays a price for everything he gets. Stringing along with Pride Seevert is the cost of peace here on the Flats."

Hannah, standing to one side, had been listening quietly. After a moment she said, "I'm glad — glad somebody's finally going to stand up to the Seeverts."

Bradford looked up at her, shook his head.

"Sounds simple when you say it, and it'd be fine to have everything all laid out neat and straight, but that's not the way it works. You give and you take."

"But mostly it's take where Pride's concerned."

The rancher sighed. "We haven't done so bad. We've all made a little money — and there's been no trouble." He paused, stared directly at Dave. "You didn't see things when they were at their worst around here. You'd already pulled out. We had a year or so of pure hell — barns burned, beef slaughtered on the range — shootings. Nobody was safe, and a man with a family — "

Hannah moved forward, placed her hand on her father's shoulder. "I'm sorry, Papa. I know what you went through — and I guess I didn't mean that the way it sounded. But I still think Pride Seevert's had his way long enough — and I'm still glad somebody's going to fight him."

Dave shifted in his chair. "I didn't come back to start a row with the Seeverts. I'm here to get my ranch started. Don't want anybody thinking wrong about that."

Hannah glanced at him and then looked down. Disappointment sobered her features.

"I'm not saying I won't fight if it's forced on me. I can't knuckle under to any man

— but I'm not looking for trouble."

Dave felt the girl's eyes on him searching, assessing, as she considered his words, sought to understand them fully. Cass Bradford, too, was silent as he gazed out across the land.

"Had two reasons for riding over here this morning," Keegan continued. "Wanted to pay my respects — and ask for your help."

The rancher leaned back, placed his empty cup on the table. Resignation settled over his face.

"Except for the land and the shacks left on it, I'm broke. To get back in the cattle business, I need cattle. I don't like to ask for credit but is there a chance you'd stake me to a starter herd — a hundred head or so? Probably be at least three years before I could pay you off, if I have no bad luck."

Very carefully and with great deliberation Cass Bradford placed his fingertips together, studied the pyramid thus formed.

"Dave — I'd like to," he said slowly. "Want you to believe that, but I reckon you know what it would mean."

"Pride Seevert?"

Bradford nodded. "Exactly. Any man who turns a hand to help you will find Seven Diamond on his back. And I — or any other rancher in the country — can't afford that.

. . . I hate it, but that's the way things are."

Dave Keegan shrugged, masking his disappointment. He got to his feet. "Was just an idea. Expect I can get some backing from — "

"I'll stake you to a herd," Hannah Bradford said abruptly.

The rancher sat up straight, alarm filling his eyes. "Now, hold on, girl — you can't — "

"Why can't I? It'll be my cattle — you gave them to me. I can do what I like with them."

"But you don't know what you'll be starting — "

"Obliged to you, Hannah," Keegan broke in. "And I appreciate the offer, but I couldn't let you do that."

The girl bristled. "Why? Are you too proud to take help from a woman? That it?"

Dave stirred. "Your pa's right. Could be the cause of big trouble."

She flashed him an angry look. "So I ought to be afraid! Well, I'm not!" she snapped, and wheeling about, stalked into the house.

Keegan watched the door close behind her. When she was gone he picked up his hat, moved to the edge of the porch, hesitated.

"Obliged for the hospitality. Appreciate it if you'll tell Hannah so for me."

Bradford rose, leaned against one of the roof supports. "Be glad to. Dave, hope you understand my position. Chances are you'd do the same was you standing in my boots."

"Maybe," Keegan said indifferently and turned toward the hitchrack. "So long."

The rancher lifted his hand. "Drop by again."

Dave nodded, but he thought, *It's not likely, knowing how you feel about the Seeverts.*

IX

Keegan pushed the buckskin to gain the crest of the rise, temper and impatience crowding him hard. He should have expected Cass Bradford to take the stand he did; Pride Seevert had everyone on the Flats buffaloed, it seemed — everyone except Pete Weems, Dutch Gooch and Hannah.

He grinned wryly as he allowed the sweaty horse to pick his way at will toward the Lazy K; a broken-down puncher, a livery stable owner — and a girl. When and if it came to a showdown with the Seeverts he'd really have some strong backing!

There'd be no *if* about it, he realized. As Cass Bradford had said, Pride Seevert could not afford a show of independence on the part of any one man; it could result in a full rebellion and the ultimate collapse of his empire. Thus he could expect Seven Diamond to act quickly.

And he would have to face them alone. Weems and Gooch, while perhaps willing, could do little. Hannah Bradford was out entirely — he would not permit her to become involved and endanger her life. What he needed was half a dozen good men, all expert with guns and imbued with the natural dislike ordinary riders have for big ranchers who have set themselves up as kings. He knew many such men but they were far away and he'd never be able to get them to the Flats in time.

Might as well face it, he told himself. *You're on your own. Is it worth it?* That question, placed to him by others, again claimed his mind. The Lazy K was a shambles. He had no cattle, and the prospects for obtaining a starter herd appeared slim. Then — why?

Dave Keegan was unsure, but it had to do with the resentment born within him long ago — ten years or so, in fact. The belief that no one man should rightfully impose his will upon another by force; the conviction that a man possessed the privilege of living, deciding and doing in accordance with his own wishes. Those were the factors shaping his determination, and while it was all slightly hazy when he tried to sort out his reasoning, he was subconsciously committed to them.

He looked ahead. The sagging buildings of the Lazy K were just beyond a knoll. Touching the buckskin with spurs, he urged him to a lope, anxious now to get home.

And then as he topped the rise, he pulled in the horse. Pete Weems was not alone. He could see others in the yard.

Drawing his gun, Keegan began to curve in from the left, walking the buckskin slowly to minimize the sound of his approach. Moments later, through a break in the bush, he caught sight of a rig — a two-seated affair hitched to a span of matched grays, standing in front of the house.

Five men hunkered in the shade. One was Weems, the others he recognized after a few moments' study: Ed Corrigan, Gower, Raskob, and Dewey Dalton. Dave holstered his pistol and rode on in, his mind filled with wonder and suspicion.

The men came to their feet when they saw him. Weems moved up to take Dave's horse, lead him back to the corral. Ed Corrigan, a thin, dark man, extended his hand.

"Good to see you, Dave."

Keegan nodded, swept the quartet with his glance. "What's this all about?"

Dalton, eyes snapping, spat impatiently. "We're here to try and talk some sense into you!"

Ed Corrigan gave the rancher an angry look. "No call for that, Dewey." He shifted his eyes to the banker. "All right, Tom."

Gower cleared his throat. "Keegan, several of us got together, held a meeting. Think maybe we've come up with a solution — one that'll be good for everybody."

"Solution to what?" Dave asked softly.

"To your coming back — wanting to start up this place again!" Dalton shouted.

"There some reason why I shouldn't run my own ranch?"

"No, naturally not," Tom Gower said hurriedly. "Only, well, let's say that maybe it's not the wisest thing for you to do."

Keegan said nothing, simply waited. Gower toyed with the gold nugget hanging from a chain looped across his vest. After a moment he continued.

"Be the best thing for you and the country. Now, we know how you feel so we've put our heads together and come up with a proposition."

Dave remained silent. Pete Weems, his chore completed, returned, squatted down, back to the wall of the house, and began to fill a blackened pipe with shreds of tobacco.

"There are some fine ranches over in the Marin River Valley country for sale. Good places a man can buy at the right price," Gower said. "We're willing to help you get your hands on one. Ride over, look at several and take your pick. Then let me know what it'll take to make a deal. I'll go along with you on a loan."

Keegan nodded slowly. He touched the other men with his glance. "That all?"

"No," Corrigan replied, "there's more. Dewey and me'll sell you a starter herd — credit of course. We're agreeable to settin' the payment up over a five year stretch — give you plenty of time to get on your feet."

"And you?" Dave pressed, placing his attention on Raskob.

Gower answered for the storekeeper. "You'll be needing supplies — food, tools, wagon and such. Raskob'll extend you all the credit you want, and you can pay him on the same basis Corrigan mentioned." The banker paused. "What do you think about it?"

"My place here — what happens to it?"

"The bank will take it over, allow you a fair price and apply it to the loan."

Dave studied the faces of the four men. Dalton, as always, was angry, belligerent; Corrigan and Tom Gower were calm, hopeful; Raskob, as if he might be regretting the generosity of an offer extending unlimited credit indefinitely, appeared worried.

"Pride Seevert put this idea into your heads?" Dave asked, finally.

Dewey Dalton took a hasty step forward

but Gower laid a hand on the redhead's shoulder, restrained him.

"No, he didn't," the banker said. "Matter of fact, we haven't seen or heard from Pride. None of us. This is our own proposition."

"He's behind it just the same," Keegan said doggedly. "You're thinking about him and how to keep him happy and satisfied — and to hell with anybody else."

"We're trying to keep this country from blowing up in our faces!" Dalton shouted.

"It's not me you ought to be worrying about!" Dave yelled back. "I'm not looking for trouble. Try working the other side of the table — call on Pride Seevert and tell him to leave me alone!"

"He'd never listen — "

"And neither will I! I've as much right here on the Flats as the Seeverts — and I intend to stay."

"It's hotheads like you that get people killed, that stir up a whole — "

"I'm not asking you or anybody else to throw in with me," Dave cut in.

"You won't have to! There's always some damned fool ready to join up at a time like this — and then we'll have hell again. Move on, Keegan. We don't want you around here. Ride out — leave us in peace!"

"The man to talk peace to," Dave replied

71

in a barely controlled voice, "is Pride Seevert, not me."

Tom Gower stepped into the heated breach. "This is getting us nowhere. Think about it, Keegan. It's a fair and sensible proposition. Nobody wants things like they once were around here. Be reasonable."

"I am — and maybe I ought to appreciate your offer, but that's a mite hard to do, knowing why you've made it. . . . But I'm staying."

"And do what?" Dalton demanded. "Hatch yourself a herd? You're broke and nobody's fool enough to lend you money or stake you to cattle. How'll you get started?"

"My problem."

Dalton muttered angrily, spun and walked to the carriage. Ed Corrigan mopped at his face.

"Your mind's made up?"

Keegan nodded. "I'll say it once more. I don't want trouble either. Man you need to talk to is Pride Seevert."

X

Dave watched the rig cut about and head for the road. He half turned as Pete Weems moved up to his side.

"Was quite a deal them jaspers offered you," the old puncher said.

Keegan shrugged. "This place is paid for — every square foot of it. I'm not about to go in over my ears for another ranch just to suit somebody else."

"Don't blame you — and it plumb tickled me to hear you tell 'em so. Was afeared there for a minute you was goin' to give in."

Dave looked closely at Weems. "Bringing the Seeverts to ground means a lot to you, doesn't it?"

The older man gazed off toward the Flats. "Reckon so — but no more'n it does to a lot of other folks. What happened at the Bradfords'?"

"Cass was friendly enough but figured he'd better play it safe. Was different with Hannah. She offered to stake me to a starter herd."

"That's fine — mighty fine! Told you she was quite a woman! When we gettin' the stock?"

"We're not."

Pete Weems stared at Dave in disbelief. "You mean you ain't takin' her up on it?"

"You know the Seeverts as well as I do — better, most likely. I won't let her get mixed up in my troubles. Too risky."

The old rider bobbed his head. "Reckon you're right. Her bein' a woman wouldn't make no difference to the Seeverts and that bunch they got workin' for them. They'd as soon crack down on her as they would a man. What comes next?"

Keegan wheeled, glanced about the yard. "Looks like you got some work done while I was gone."

"Sure did. That there wire's been strung, like you wanted. Acrost every foot around the place, 'ceptin' the road comin' in. Got a piece handy there we can put up at night. And the corral's fixed."

Dave nodded his approval. "Place's starting to look like something."

"All we're needin' is cows."

"We'll get 'em. Aim to start for Junction City about dark."

"How long you be gone?"

"Three days, likely. What about that cook

you mentioned?"

"Joe Henley?"

"Never told me his name. Can you get him?"

"Sure. Seen him when I went after that load of grub. Said he'd be right pleased to take the job. He ain't got no hankerin' for the Seeverts either. Used to work for 'em but somethin' happened and they up and give him his time. Want me to fetch him?"

"Long as he knows how things stand out here."

"That'll make him want the job more'n ever. He sure hates them Seeverts after what they done to him. Joe's kind of up in years, like me, and he ain't been able to get work nowhere."

"About all it'll amount to will be cooking chores and the like."

"He'll jump at the chance. When you want him?"

"Now — today. Don't think it's smart to leave one man here alone."

" 'Spect you're right. I'll be linin' out for town right away, then. Anythin' you're needin'?"

"Nothing," Dave said, and added, "Keep your eye out for that bushwhacker."

Weems, turning away for the corral, paused, seemed about to say something. He thought better of it, merely nodded and went on.

Keegan waited until he had ridden out of the yard and then entered the house. Going through the supplies on the shelves, he selected what he would need for the trail and placed it on the table. Obtaining his saddlebags from the buckskin, in the corral where Weems had loosed him, he carried them back to the house and loaded the pockets. When that was done and he had filled his canteen with fresh water, he looked around for something to do while he waited for the return of Weems and Joe Henley.

The tool shed. They'd be needing a place to accumulate the various implements and keep them where they'd be handy. He went out into the yard behind the house, crossed to the small, square structure, fortunately still upright. The roof had blown off, lay a few steps beyond.

Hoisting it into place, Dave obtained the hammer and handful of nails, secured it. The leather hinges on the door had rotted through. Locating another piece, a remnant of a discarded trace, he cut new lengths, reset the warped panel and affixed the wire latch. He began then to collect the tools, those left by his father and the new ones supplied by Dutch Gooch, and stack them inside where they would be out of the weather.

The job took little more than an hour and he looked around for something else to occupy his time. He was trying to keep busy and giving little thought to the visit paid him by Gower and the others. But now Dewey Dalton's words came back to him: *Hothead,* the rancher had called him. *Get people killed,* he had said.

Keegan considered that. Was he a hothead because he wanted to run his ranch in his own way? As for getting others hurt — he was asking no one to side in with him. Pete Weems had asked for the job — seemed anxious to get it. And Henley; he would have a clear understanding of what it was all about.

As to other ranchers, so far none had made their intentions to join with him known. Of course he could hear from some of them later; word had hardly had time to get around. If there were some who felt as he did, it would be because they wanted to make a stand against Pride Seevert, not because he asked or encouraged them to. Could he be blamed because they were fed up with paying through the nose to the Seeverts?

Hardly. It would be their own decision, and if they threw in with him they would do so fully aware of what it meant. He'd see to that. But he doubted if there would be many who —

The loud rattle of loose pebbles in a tin can brought Dave Keegan's thoughts to a sudden halt. Someone had blundered into the low-strung wire. The sound came again, almost immediately — and from the opposite side of the yard.

Dave stepped back against the tool shed. His hand dropped to the pistol on his hip, froze as a sharp voice laid a warning across the quiet.

"Forget it, Keegan!"

A moment later Pride Seevert rode into view.

XI

Cursing himself for his carelessness, Dave allowed his arms to fall. He should have known better — he should have been on his guard. Motion to the left caught his eye. Chancy — moving in slowly, gun in hand. And on the right brother Gabe, husky, sullen-faced, following a like pattern. They had him pinned from three sides.

He brought his attention back to Pride, now halted a few paces in front of him. The eldest Seevert had changed little: a bit older, perhaps, but the same tight mouth, cold blue eyes and beak-like nose. Watching intently, he settled back, waited for Chancy and Gabe to complete their chore.

Tom Gower and the others had lost no time getting word to Pride, Keegan thought, and then realized such would have been impossible. Less than two hours had elapsed since the men pulled out of the yard; likely they were still on their way to town. The banker, the merchant, and the two ranchers had been acting on their own behalf, just as they'd insisted.

"Get his gun."

Chancy's harsh voice registered on his consciousness. He drew back, preparing himself for what he was certain the next few minutes would bring. There was a lessening of weight on his hip as Gabe lifted the Colt from its holster — and then he buckled forward as Chancy drove his knotted fist deep into his belly.

"Here — none of that! Don't want it looking like there was a fight around here!"

Pride Seevert's words seemed to come from a far distance. Dave, gasping for breath, straightened slowly. Chancy, grinning broadly, posed before him.

"Owed me that — and plenty more."

"Maybe so," Pride answered, "but this ain't the place — or the time. Get a rope around him."

Keegan felt a loop drop around him, cinch tight, pinning his arms to his sides. He faced the elder Seevert squarely.

"Roughing me up won't change anything."

"You made that plain to Chancy," Pride answered. "Don't figure to waste any more time on you."

Understanding came to Keegan. He nodded. "Explains why you haven't got half a dozen of your hired hands along. Don't want them seeing you commit murder."

Seevert shrugged. "You had your chance — twice. Instead of taking it, you wanted to play it hard-nosed. All right. We'll do things your way."

"You're overshooting the mark this time. Had some visitors here less'n two hours ago. Anything happens to me they'll know you had a hand in it. Even they won't stand for cold-blooded murder."

"They'll stand for anything," Seevert said with a half smile. "Besides — who said anything about murder? You're just going to disappear."

"Nobody'll swallow that one either."

"You sure of that? All I've got to do is show a bill of sale for this place and say you rode on. They'll believe it."

"There are a dozen men who know I won't sell. You try convincing them — "

"Won't even bother," Pride cut in. "They know better'n to question me. . . . Gabe, get that horse of his saddled and ready to ride."

"You're takin' a little trip," Chancy said coyly, prodding Dave sharply with his pistol. "One you won't be comin' back from. Ever hear of Hell Canyon?"

"I've heard of it," Keegan snapped angrily, "and if you jab that goddam gun barrel into me once more, I'll stomp you into the ground — no matter what!"

Chancy fell back a step. Pride laughed quietly. Over in the corral Gabe mumbled irritably as he threw gear onto the buckskin.

"Talk mighty tough for a man about to take his last ride," Chancy said, recovering his bravado.

"Not over yet," Dave said, thinking of the canyon. It was a short, very narrow and deep cleft in the mountains just off a wall of towering palisades. A veritable trap because of its sheer walls, it had meant doom for countless wild animals, straying stock and an occasional unwary rider.

"Was about to take your pa on the same ride," Chancy went on, "when he up and died. Saved us the trouble."

Keegan's eyes pulled into slits. "What the hell were you picking on him for? He was going along with you and your highbinding deal."

"At first," Pride Seevert said, coming into the conversation. "Then he got lazy — or maybe too old to do his ranching. Just quit. Wanted to get rid of him so's I could put somebody there who'd work — raise cattle. Like Chancy said, he died, solved the problem."

Dave Keegan was trembling with fury.

"Expect you helped things on a little."

"Guess maybe we did," Chancy said, shaking his head. "Old buzzard was sort of hard-nosed. Can see where you get it."

Temper roared through Keegan. Forgetting the rope that bound his arms, he hurled himself at Seevert. His shoulder caught the man in the chest, bowled him over. Pride yelled, spurred forward. Dave saw him coming, saw the pistol in his hand lifted as a club. He dodged to one side, took the blow high on his arm.

In the next instant Chancy was back on his feet, rushing in. Keegan whirled again, striving to protect himself. The youngest Seevert caught him flush on the chin with a hard right. Dave felt his senses waver. A second blow to the side of his head dropped him to his knees. He hung there, helpless, wavering uncertainly.

"That's enough!" Pride's voice said.

Pain shot anew through Keegan's body as Chancy drove a boot into his back. He felt himself slipping sideways.

"I'll kill him!" Chancy's words were high-pitched, almost a scream. "I'll kill the bastard!"

"Grab him, Gabe!"

Prone in the dust, Dave's head began to clear. Through a faint haze he saw Gabe wrap his thick arms around his younger brother, bodily lift him off his feet and set him aside.

"You heard Pride — cut it out!"

Keegan fought himself to a sitting position. Pain was shooting through his kidneys and cobwebs still cluttered his mind.

"Throw some water on him," Pride ordered.

Gabe obtained the bucket from the kitchen, dashed its contents against Dave's sweat-coated face. The shock brought him around instantly. He shook his head, got slowly to his feet. Chancy stood in his direct line of vision.

"Damn you," he muttered and lunged again.

Gabe, holding to the rope around Keegan's middle, brought him up short. Chancy laughed, swaggered forward a few paces.

"Good thing he stopped you. Was all set to knock your — "

"Bring that horse up here!" Pride shouted impatiently. "We ain't got time to set around here while you show off what a big man you are."

Chancy paused, threw a look at his older brother and then shambled over to where the buckskin waited. Gabe, taking a couple of hitches in the rope that bound Keegan, jerked him around to where he could mount.

"I'm fixin' this," he said, "so's I can yank you right off'n the saddle if you try somethin' cute . . . Put your foot in that there stirrup."

Leaning to one side Dave managed to anchor his boot toe in the wooden opening. Gabe immediately seized him about the waist, swung him onto the hull. Handing the buckskin's reins to Pride, he turned to get his own mount.

"What're you waiting on?" the elder Seevert asked, glaring at Chancy. "You want Gabe to help you up, too?"

Chancy swore angrily, spun and strode to where his horse stood.

Pride glanced at Dave, wagged his head. "Reckon I ought to just turn him loose on you, let him have himself a time. Do him good, maybe."

"Better wrap another rope around me if you do," Keegan said coolly. "I get half a chance, I'll kill him."

"Expect you would at that," Pride answered, and turned to face Gabe and Chancy riding into the yard. "Everything ready?"

Gabe bobbed his head. Pride looked around the yard. "Like I said, I don't want it looking like there was a scrap here."

"Ought to burn the damned place — right to the ground," Chancy said sourly.

"Be a fool thing to do — burn our own holdings. Belongs to us now."

The younger Seevert grinned. "Yeah, I forgot about that."

"I'll lead off," Pride continued. "Put Keegan in behind me — then you, Gabe. We'll head straight for the palisades."

"What about me?" Chancy asked, frowning.

"You trot along back of Gabe, keep your eyes peeled on the Flats in case somebody starts trailing us. You see somebody, sing out. Understand?"

"Sure, Pride, only I'd ruther look after Keegan, keep him humpin' along."

"Gabe'll take care of him. Need you to do the watchin'. Sooner we get this trouble-maker and his horse dumped into the bottom of Hell Canyon, better I'll like it."

Chancy laughed. "Me too," he said.

XII

They moved off, Pride leading them immediately into the dense tamarisk windbreak bordering the north side of the yard where they were quickly out of sight. Seevert veered then to the west, following a well-beaten cattle trail that pointed in a direct line for Tenkiller Mountain.

Keegan moved his arms slightly, experimentally. The rope encircled him with two loops and had been drawn tight. Gabe was maintaining tautness by steady pressure that permitted no slack in the line. One thing was in his favor: they had not tied his hands, and that offered hope.

He looked ahead, calculating his chances. Pride was ten feet or so in front of him, leaning forward on the saddle, eyes on the distant slopes. Gabe Seevert was a like distance behind, a squat, solid uncommunicative man with an expressionless face. Fifty yards beyond him Chancy brought up the rear of the little column.

To simply make a break for it was out

of the question. Gabe had his end of the rope anchored firmly to the horn of his saddle, thus preventing any sudden flight. And even if he were fortunate enough to escape the rope, Pride and the others would shoot him down before he could get a dozen paces.

Grim, he raked his brain for another idea; there had to be some avenue, some means of breaking free. He just couldn't sit quiet and let them lead him off to slaughter without a fight. But he would have to come up with something soon; already they had reached the first gentle slopes of the mountain, and were picking their way along a narrow path.

He glanced at the sun: mid-afternoon. Pete Weems and his friend Henley had likely returned to the ranch by that hour. They would wonder what had happened to him. Pete would then discover his saddlebags, loaded for the trip to Junction City, on the table, realize immediately that something was wrong. But he would do nothing for the simple reason that there was nothing he could do. Keegan swore deeply as tension built steadily within him; there was nothing anyone could do for him — he was strictly on his own.

Again he tried the rope. His arms, numbed by their bonds, moved slightly. Hope stirred as he realized the irregularity of the trail was making it hard for Gabe to keep the line taut. It was a small encouragement and opened up no specific possibilities but he worked covertly at increasing the slack, nevertheless.

Time wore on, hot and silent, and with it dragged the slow miles. The trail grew steeper and the horses began to lather and suck for wind. Pride Seevert did not pause but pressed on as if reaching their destination at the earliest moment was of prime importance.

Keegan wondered at that. Was Seevert afraid of encountering someone? It didn't seem likely, as they were now directly west of Seven Diamond range and the only persons in the area would be their own hired hands. There was some other reason, he finally concluded, but he could think of nothing logical.

They topped out a rise in the trail, swung to the left. The gray, ragged walls of the palisades reared before them. Dave's nerves tightened. Hell Canyon was less than a mile distant. Every passing moment now was putting him closer to his last breath.

He pressed harder against the rope, felt it give as the knot slipped. A little more and he'd be able to hook his thumbs under the hemp loops and throw them over his head. Then what? He studied Pride Seevert's hunched shape. His best chance lay there — digging spurs into the buckskin, sending him straight ahead. He'd try to knock Pride off his saddle as he raced by, hope Gabe would hesitate to shoot for fear of hitting his brother. Chancy was too far back to be a problem.

Keegan bowed his elbows again, pushed once more against the rope. The loops gave easily, slid downward an inch or two.

"Hey — what the hell you doin'?"

Gabe's raspy voice shattered the silence as he hauled back on the rope savagely. Keegan felt the coils tighten around his middle, almost jerk him from his seat. Pride stopped short, looked back, and there was a quick pound of hooves as Chancy hurried up.

"What's goin' on?"

"Tryin' to shuck out of my lasso, that's what," Gabe said. "Real cute."

Pride said, "Watch him close. We're almost there. . . . Chancy, you better side Gabe — just in case."

"He won't be tryin' nothin' again," Gabe promised as the column resumed.

Keegan rode in silence. His one chance, however slim, had vanished. There was nothing left now but to wait it out, hope, for a last moment opportunity.

Abruptly Pride halted. Standing in his stirrups, he stared down a gentle slope the end of which was marked by a low hedge of snakeweed, sage and other stunted growth. The lip of the canyon, Keegan realized.

"Good a place as any," Seevert said, settling back on the saddle. "Gabe, bring him over here, put him below us. Chancy, give your brother a hand there."

"You wantin' him on his horse?"

"Of course I want him on his horse! You think I want any boot tracks showing around here?"

Chancy muttered something, moved up to Keegan and took a firm grip on the buckskin's bridle. Spurring his own horse, he led Dave's mount to a point halfway between Pride and the edge of the canyon.

"Right here suit you, mister?" Chancy asked, his tone sarcastic.

"Good," Pride answered, undisturbed. "Now come up here next to me while Gabe gets that rope off'n him."

The plan was clear to Dave Keegan. The Seeverts were trapping him between them and the canyon. At a given signal all would rush him, haze the buckskin over the edge to certain death on the rocks far below. When — if ever — his body was found it would appear an unfortunate accident ended his life.

Tense, he waited while Gabe, keeping at a safe distance, shook the rope free and flipped it clear. He could make a run for it but he knew in advance such would end in failure. Pride would use a gun if forced to — and it would be easy to down the buckskin when he tried to cross in front of them. Likely they would then knock him unconscious and throw him over the rim. It would still look like an accident.

He watched Gabe move up-grade and wheel in beside Pride, coiling his rope as he did. The older Seevert drew his pistol, pointed it skyward.

"All right — you boys ready?"

Chancy and Gabe had their weapons out. Pride said, "Now, be damn sure you don't hit him — or the horse."

Gabe nodded. Chancy, his face glistening with sweat, eyes bright, simply waited. Keegan, crouched low, touched the buckskin lightly with his spurs, started him walking slowly across the grade. He had no plan, no thought as to how he might avoid the charge; he could only face it on a moment to moment basis.

"Get him!" Pride yelled and, pressing off a shot, drove his barbs into the flank of his horse.

All three riders, yelling and shooting, instantly swept down the short slope. At the first report Keegan brought the buckskin around sharply, started him directly upgrade. The gunshot, the yelling and the oncoming horses brought him to his back legs. He wheeled in mid-air, came down solidly, began to stampede toward the lip of the canyon.

Keegan sawed at the reins, succeeded in turning him half around. Abruptly the Seeverts were on him, yelling, shooting, crowding him toward the rim, Dave lashed out at the nearest, Gabe, struck the man a glancing blow on the head. He had the buckskin pointed uphill again, was goading him cruelly with his spurs.

"Push him over — push him over!" Pride Seevert yelled.

Dave had a brief glimpse of Chancy, lips pulled back in a tight grin, rushing straight for him. He drove spurs home again, slapped the buckskin sharply on the neck. The horse wheeled, lunged away. Chancy thundered by, and collided solidly with Gabe. Both mounts went down, thrashing wildly. Keegan, fighting the buckskin, found himself behind the Seeverts, in the clear. He leaned forward and goaded the animal into a straightaway run for the trail.

Reaching it, he looked back. One of the

horses had gone over the edge. Pride and Chancy were on their knees, assisting Gabe, who also had lost his footing but had managed to arrest his fall by grabbing onto the weeds that lined the brink of the canyon.

XIII

The buckskin was tired but Keegan held him to a steady lope down the trail. That there would be pursuit he was certain — just which of the Seevert brothers it would be was the only question. Most likely Chancy, Dave decided. With only two horses between the three of them, it was logical to assume Pride would take Gabe with him, riding double, back to Seven Diamond while he sent the youngest Seevert to finish the job they had started.

And this time it would be no cunningly devised plan designed to leave no trace, no evidence. Pride's instructions would be to kill, employing any means and opportunity available.

A gun — he must get a gun. He considered that, concluded his best bet was to return to the Lazy K, despite the fact that the Seeverts would undoubtedly look there first for him. But he had a spare six-gun in the few belongings he had brought — an old, bone-handled forty-five with a hair trigger given to him years back by a friend. Once he had a weapon with which to defend himself, he could decide what his next move should be.

The buckskin began to heave and he pulled the horse in to a trot. Turning his head he listened into the fading day. Faintly, above the drum of his own horse, he could hear the hollow beat of an oncoming rider. He hadn't guessed wrong: one of the Seeverts was trailing him.

Dave looked ahead. He was almost to the foot of the mountain. Once off the narrow, winding path and on the wooded slopes it wouldn't be hard to shake the pursuit. He glanced at the sun. Still a couple of hours, at least, until darkness. No help there.

The end of the trail appeared abruptly. He broke out onto the barren knoll, veered hard right for a thick stand of piñon trees. The buckskin had to rest, if only for a few moments. Halting well back from the base of the mountain, he waited behind the screen of foliage. The tattoo of beating hooves was much louder and he realized that Seevert had gained on him during the descent. If the trail had lasted for another mile or two he would have found himself a target for gunshots.

Abruptly a rider swept around the last

bend and raced into view. It was Chancy, crouched low and flogging his horse unmercifully for more speed. Dave watched him race out into the open, continue without hesitation along the main path up which they had all ridden earlier. Chancy had jumped to a conclusion; he was assuming that Keegan would ride straight to the Lazy K.

Dave allowed the buckskin to rest for a quarter hour and then moved on, taking a southerly direction until he was a full mile below the route Seevert had taken, and then swung east. Chancy would eventually discover his error and back-track; unarmed, Dave Keegan was taking precautions to avoid an encounter.

He reached the Lazy K well after dark. There were no lights showing and he halted in the tamarisk outside the yard while he studied the weathered buildings thoughtfully. Where were Pete and Joe Henley?

After a few minutes he dismounted, secured the buckskin to a stout clump, and walked through the shadows until he was directly opposite the house. Again he paused, listened.

Somewhere, back in the direction of Tenkiller Mountain, a coyote was barking. Insects clacked in the night, and off to his right there was a dry rustling in the leaves as a field mouse, or some small creature, scurried about. And then from inside the house Keegan heard the low, muted sound of a man's voice. Weems and Henley were there, evidently on guard.

"Pete!" he called softly.

There was no answer. Dave cupped his hands to his lips. "Pete — it's me, Keegan."

A hinge screeched faintly. Weems's high-pitched tones cautiously probed the darkness. "Dave — that you?"

"It's me. I'm coming in."

Keegan crossed the yard in half a dozen hurried strides and entered the house. "What's this all about?"

The old puncher closed the door, struck a match to the lantern. He waved carelessly at an elderly man sitting beneath a window, a shotgun across his knees.

"That there's Joe Henley — feller I was tellin' you about."

Dave nodded to the newcomer. "Why are you all forted up? Something happen?"

"Was somebody out there awhile ago. Didn't hear 'em come, but heard 'em go. Wasn't takin' no chances, seein' as how you just up and disappeared sudden-like. Where in tarnation you been?"

"With the Seeverts — at Hell Canyon," Dave replied, stepping to his bunk. Unrolling a bundle, he obtained the bone-handled forty-five, flipped open the loading gate and began to insert cartridges into the cylinder.

Weems was staring at him. "What the devil you doin' up there?"

"Seems to be their private burying ground — for people they don't want around," Keegan said and related what had taken place. "That probably was Chancy you heard outside, looking for me."

Pete Weems was nodding slowly. "Expect, was we to climb down into that canyon, we'd find some of them folks that just dropped out of sight. Could explain a whole lot of things." He paused, watched as Dave slid the pistol into his holster. "What're you aimin' to do? Pride ain't goin' to let you run loose, knowin' what you do now."

"My thinking hasn't got that far yet. One thing I'd like to ask you — my pa ever tell you he'd been beat up by the Seeverts?"

Pete clawed at his chin. "Don't recollect him ever sayin' so."

"He ever look like it?"

The old puncher frowned. "Well, maybe there was a couple o' times it could've been that. Rode by here once and he was all banged up and hobblin' about. Said he'd fell off'n his horse. Remember thinkin' it was the wrong kind of bungin' up for that. Face was all swole and both eyes was black. Why?"

Keegan's voice was taut with anger. "The Seeverts were trying to force him off his land."

"You sayin' they beat him up?"

Dave nodded slowly. "Chancy dropped the word that his dying saved them from taking him up to the Canyon when they couldn't make him do what they wanted."

Joe Henley swore harshly. "Day's comin' when somebody'll take care of them Seeverts!"

Dave's hand dropped to the curved handle of his weapon. "The day's here," he murmured.

XIV

Henley asked, "How you goin' to do it? The Seeverts are a big outfit."

There was a thread of doubt in the man's tone. Weems, eyes bright, was grinning broadly.

"Don't you worry none about Dave, here! Seen him take on Chancy and his crowd twice now. He can handle them — the whole dang push!"

"Chancy's one thing. Pride and Gabe are somethin' else."

"Don't make no difference to Dave!" Weems, glowing like fanned embers, wheeled to Keegan. "What're you figurin' to do — pay 'em a little visit?"

"Won't need to. They'll be looking for me."

"And you'll be settin' here — waitin'."

Keegan made no comment. Henley stood his shotgun against the wall, reached into his pocket for a plug of tobacco.

"Man's got a right to defend his property. You takin' them on alone? Nobody comin' to help?"

101

"Nobody," Dave said. "Expect you two'd better head back for town in the morning. Anybody the Seeverts see hanging around me they'll figure's against them, too."

Henley gnawed off a corner of the plug, shifted it into the hollow of his cheek. "Thought you was tryin' to stir up some help against them."

"Maybe I was, at the start, but I got to thinking about it. Wrong thing for me to do, talk people into fighting, getting themselves shot up, their places burned. I'm the one who's not satisfied. Makes it my problem."

"Well, I ain't pullin' out!" Weems declared. "I been honin' for a crack at Pride Seevert!"

Joe Henley leaned back, bobbed his head thoughtfully. "You got yourself a powerful hate for Pride 'cause of what he done to you. Reckon that goes for you both. Now take me — the Seeverts done me dirt in another way, and I ain't forgettin' it. Howsomever, there's still more to it. Them and their kind is ruinin' this whole country — and that's somethin' I can't abide! Way I see it, any man ought to rise right up and do his share when it's time to start skinnin' snakes."

Pete Weems stared at his friend. "All that windy palaver — that mean you're of a notion to help?"

"It does," Henley said.

"Obliged to both of you," Keegan said, "but I'm not sure you understand what you'll be up against. The Seeverts don't just plan to run me out of the country. Way it stands now they've got to get rid of me for good. You side me, you'll be in the same wagon."

"Ain't tellin' me somethin' I don't know," Pete said.

"Me neither," Henley added. "What the hell — man can't expect to keep on livin' forever. . . . Anything special we ought to be doin'?"

Dave was silent for a long moment, and then he smiled. "We shouldn't be holed up in here, that's for damn sure! Be a trap if the Seeverts hit us tonight."

"Where can we go?" Weems wondered.

"Out in the brush. Grab up a couple of blankets. We'll pick a place where we can keep an eye on the yard."

"How about grub? You ain't et yet, have you?"

Keegan reached for his saddlebags, still on the table. "Can make out with what's in here. There coffee in that pot?"

Pete stepped to the stove, tested the weight of the blackened granite utensil. "Nigh half full."

"That'll hold us until morning," Keegan

said. "Let's move."

They settled on a low rise just west of the yard. It was densely covered with rabbit brush, stray clumps of tamarisk brought in by the wind, scrub oak and mountain mahogany. By parting the thick foliage they had a good view of the house and yard — as well as the far side, which was the direction the Seeverts would most likely come in from.

He doubted very much, however, that they would see anything of the Seven Diamond crowd before morning. Chancy, failing to find Dave at his ranch, would have then returned to the Seevert place and rejoined his brothers. After that would come the planning, during which Pride would set forth what had to be done. All of this would require time.

They made themselves comfortable and Keegan, after eating from the supplies in his saddlebag and drinking two cups of the still warm coffee, lay back, suddenly aware of his weariness and the need for sleep. He dozed immediately, unmindful of the voices of Weems and Henley as they argued amiably over some trivial matter.

He awoke to find them already up and about. Henley had made a trip to the house and returned with a frying pan, a section from the side of bacon and some potatoes he had thoughtfully put in the stove's oven that previous afternoon. Weems had a small fire going and the coffee ready.

He greeted Dave with a cup of the steaming black liquid and smiled. "You sure been poundin' your ear!"

"Didn't know I was so beat," Keegan answered, thanking the old man. He glanced at the sun, commented, "Pretty late."

"Was just about to roust you out. Company ought to be comin' pretty quick. We stayin' here?"

Keegan nodded. "Good a place as any. Expect we ought to bring the horses over, have them handy." He drained his cup, set it on a rock near the fire. "We can do that while Joe's fixing breakfast."

Together he and Weems walked to the corral where their mounts had been placed, and after throwing on the gear, led them to the rear of the thicket. When they rejoined Henley he had their plates well filled with slices of fried bacon and browned potatoes. He grinned at Dave.

"They always give a condemned man a hearty meal. Figured we was entitled to the same treatment."

There could be considerable truth in the words, Keegan thought, finding himself a place to sit. He wished it were possible to

105

settle things with the Seeverts without blood-shed, but such seemed out of the question. After what had happened that previous day there wasn't any other answer. One thing he was glad of: he hadn't dragged any other rancher into the showdown. He was in it alone except for Pete and Joe Henley — and they had their own private reasons for taking a hand.

"Somebody comin'!"

Pete Weems's warning brought him to his feet instantly. He had heard nothing, but there was no reason to doubt the old puncher. Setting his plate aside, he felt for his pistol and then moved to the front of the screening shrubbery. He caught the sound then — the quiet thud of approaching horses.

Keegan frowned. He had expected the Seeverts to appear on the opposite side of the yard. Seven Diamond lay in that direction. These riders were coming in on their left.

"Watch sharp!" he said quietly. "They could be all around us."

Earlier he hadn't considered the possibility — that of finding themselves surrounded. It seemed more likely that Pride and the others would strike head-on.

"Hello, the house!"

At the summons Dave Keegan stiffened. He doubled back through the brush, looking to the source of the call.

"Ain't any of Pride's bunch," Pete Weems said. "Sounds like Cass Bradford."

"That's who it is," Keegan replied in a falling voice. "He's got Hannah with him."

XV

"Sure the wrong time for them to be showin' up," Weems muttered. "What you reckon they want?"

Dave stepped into the open. Immediately the rancher and his daughter angled toward him. Hannah was smiling faintly but Bradford, sensing something was amiss, held a straight face. They halted in front of Keegan and swung down.

"Trouble?"

Dave nodded slowly to the rancher's question.

Bradford asked, "The Seeverts?"

Again Keegan moved his head. "Had a run-in with them yesterday."

"Bad?"

"Bad enough," Dave said, skipping details. "Don't think you and Hannah ought to be found here."

Instantly the girl bristled. "Neither Pride Seevert nor anybody else can tell us what we can do — " she began angrily, and then fell silent as her father lifted his hand.

"Don't guess it'll make much difference, anyway," he said resignedly. "Rode by to tell you we'd moved a hundred head of beef onto your south range. Starter herd. After you left yesterday Hannah convinced me it was the thing to do."

"About the worst — far as you're concerned," Keegan said. "Pride's taken it into his head to crack down on me. Same thing'll hold for my friends."

"You mean you don't want the cattle?" Hannah demanded.

"Of course I want them, and I'm obliged to you for giving me a hand. But with the Seeverts — "

"The Seeverts!" Hannah echoed. "I'm sick of hearing about them! Why are you all so afraid of that bunch? They're just men. If I had a gun — "

"Now, hold on!" Keegan broke in harshly, temper finally getting the best of him. "Being a woman, maybe you've got a right to speak out that way, but that kind of talk's going to get somebody killed — most likely your pa. Let me give you a little advice: stay out of this — keep your lip buttoned."

Hannah flushed hotly and looked down. Cass Bradford slanted a glance at his daughter, grinned slightly, and then brought his attention back to Keegan.

"See now I should've done some talkin' before I had the boys drive those steers over. But they're here. Ain't much we can do to change that."

"Still a way out," Dave said. "You two get off my land fast as you can. Don't let any of the Seven Diamond outfit see you."

"But the cattle . . ."

"If the Seeverts spot them I'll say they drifted over the line onto my range — that I've sent word to you to come get them."

Bradford nodded. "Just might work."

"Feared it won't," Joe Henley said from the depths of the brush. "We got company right now."

Keegan wheeled in alarm, threw his glance to the far side of the yard. All three Seeverts, with half a dozen riders flanking them, were strung out along the windbreak. He could see more Seven Diamond hired hands moving in the brush.

"Circlin' us," Weems said. "Like a bunch of Injuns."

"Pull back!" Dave said hurriedly. "Don't think they've seen — "

A pistol shot cracked sharply. The sound of a bullet clipping through foliage just above his head caused Keegan to duck involuntarily. Cursing, he dragged out his gun, then paused. He could make no stand there — not with

Hannah Bradford with him.

"Keegan!"

It was Pride Seevert's voice. Dave motioned the others deeper into the brush where the horses waited.

"Keegan — I know you're holed up in there. We've got you cold — but I'm willing to give you one more chance. Come out with your hands up and we'll talk sense."

Dave looked over his shoulder. The Bradfords and Henley had reached the horses. Pete Weems had halted, was staring at him.

"You ain't swallerin' that, are you? Only talkin' Pride'll do will be with that gun he's holdin'. He just plain can't afford to let you keep on livin'."

Keegan said, "Know that. Go on with the others. Take my horse — lead them all straight back. I'll follow. Got to get out of here before we're surrounded."

Weems was staring beyond him at the men on the far side of the yard. His lean, hawk-like face was set and his eyes burned fiercely.

"Could easy blast that goddam Pride off'n his saddle from here," he murmured.

"And have them open up on us with every gun they've got? We've got Hannah to think about — and her pa."

The old puncher's shoulders slumped.

"Reckon you're right. Wouldn't make no difference to the Seeverts. What're you figurin' to do?"

"Move out of here before it turns into a trap. Lead the others, like I told you, straight back. Brush runs for a couple of hundred yards — ends at a dry wash. Once we've reached that, we can make a run for the mountains."

"Keegan!"

Dave turned, hopeful that Pete Weems had understood; he could ignore Pride Seevert no longer.

"I hear you!" he shouted.

"You comin' out?"

It was Chancy this time. He cast a quick look over his shoulder. Weems, followed by Hannah and her father, and with Henley bringing up the rear, were disappearing into the thick growth.

"Thinking it over," he replied, glancing to the sides. He could see nothing to his left, but to the right he caught sight of a rider winding in and out of the brush. They were closing the circle. Dave smiled grimly. Both he and Pride Seevert were playing a game of delay: he holding back until Weems and the others were out of danger, Pride striving to occupy him while his men slipped in and formed a ring.

"Thinkin' over what?" Chancy yelled. "One way or another you're comin' out of there!"

Keegan once again turned away. Weems and his party were out of sight — and beyond the approaching rider.

"Guess you're right," he answered.

Removing his hat, he perched it on a low stump in front of a thick clump of oak brush. Then, crouched low, he wheeled and began to make his way toward the point where he had last seen Weems and the others.

He had taken no more than a dozen steps when a sound to his left brought him to a dead stop. Peering through the shrubbery he saw another of Seevert's men, the one he had failed to locate earlier, working in. The Seven Diamond rider was on foot, leading his mount. Keegan grinned. The man would pass within a long stride; it would be easy to move swiftly, club him to the ground with no one being the wiser.

Dave throttled the impulse. The second rider would see the unattended horse, immediately suspect something was wrong and set up an alarm. His scheme for an escape depended on keeping the Seeverts and their men concentrating on the brush where he, supposedly, was hiding. The planted hat, he felt, should prolong that belief.

Scarcely breathing, he watched the man walk by, and then quiet as smoke, he hurried to overtake the others.

XVI

The trail was dim, all but wiped out by ten years of encroaching underbrush, yet he followed it with no difficulty. Countless times as a boy he had made his way along the path as part of a shortcut leading eventually to the mountains, and now he was taking it again. But on this day it was for a different reason and under desperate circumstances.

He reached the arroyo, dropped to its sandy floor where the others awaited him, went straight to his buckskin, and vaulted to the saddle.

"Stay close to me," he said, and spurred forward.

Stilled by the tautness of his manner, the rest of the party swung in behind him and in a close, compact column, headed up the wash.

Almost immediately a shout lifted from the brush where they had hidden.

"He ain't here!"

Pride Seevert's voice bellowed a reply. "What do you mean he ain't there?"

"Tricked us — with his damned hat!"

Dave swore quietly. He had hoped to gain more time, and thus a better start, but his ruse had been discovered quickly. He glanced back at those following him. Hannah's features were strained; the faces of the men were set, grim. He wondered if the girl realized, as did the men, the seriousness of their position. If so, she betrayed no fear at the prospects.

"Keep up!" he called over his shoulder, and dug his spurs into the buckskin.

The horse broke into a lope. It was punishment for the animals, he knew, laboring up-grade in the loose sand of the wash, but they could not afford to let the Seeverts get within gunshot. He looked again to the rear. The Seven Diamond men had not yet found the trail to enter the arroyo. *Luck's with us so far,* Keegan thought.

The buckskin began to heave, his wind going fast on the tough climb. Dave stared ahead, calculating distance. Still a good quarter mile to the bend in the wash where they could climb out and be on firm ground. He eased up on the horse, allowed him to drop into a trot.

"Good thing," he heard Pete Weems say in a grumbling voice. "Nag o' mine's about done for."

Keegan made no reply, simply held the buckskin to the pace. He could see the slope leading up from the arroyo. Snakeweed had found purchase in the hard clay and it was almost covered. Erosion, too, had left its scarring mark but it appeared ascendable.

He drew abreast the bend, veered the horse for the sharp grade. The buckskin slowed, gathered his muscles and lunged. His hooves stabbed into the baked soil, churned furiously, and then abruptly he was on the top. Keegan wheeled him around, halted on the level ground. While the others followed the trail dug by the buckskin, he threw his glance toward the lower end of the wash.

There was no sign of the Seevert party, but that could mean nothing. The arroyo whipped back and forth many times during its course to the lower flats, effectively cutting off the view of anyone hoping to see for any distance.

Bradford paused beside him. "Think we shook them?"

Dave shrugged. "Doubt it. Pride'll realize there was only one way out of that trap — south. He'll have his look and when he gets to the arroyo there'll be plenty of tracks to follow."

"Hadn't we better keep goin' then?"

"Got to give the horses a breather. Five

minutes'll mean a lot to them — not much where Seevert's bunch is concerned."

"Where does this trail lead?" Hannah asked, looking off into the brush.

"To the lower end of the mountain," Dave replied. "We'll come to a fork about a quarter mile this side. Want you and your pa to take the left-hand. It'll put you on Ed Corrigan's place, get you out of this."

"You and the others heading up onto the mountain?" Bradford said.

Keegan nodded. "Figure we can give them the slip there. If we don't there'll be plenty of good places where we can make a stand. . . . Let's move out."

He cut the buckskin around and pointed him up the narrow path, scarcely visible in the thick growth. The others fell in behind him, maintaining a close column. When they reached the point where the brush cut off a final glimpse of the arroyo, Keegan looked back. Pride Seevert and his Seven Diamond men were just coming into view. Dave stiffened involuntarily. Weems, watching him at the moment, turned, followed his gaze.

"Sure didn't take 'em long," the old puncher said grimly. "Reckon we can outrun 'em?"

Keegan said, "We've got to," and urged the buckskin to a lope.

An hour later, with the horses laboring under the strain, they reached the split in the trail. The Seeverts had trimmed their lead some but they were still a safe distance to the rear. Dave faced Bradford and his daughter.

"We're leaving you here," he said, ducking his head toward the path that led directly to the mountain. "You ride south. Corrigan's ranch is six, maybe seven miles."

Cass Bradford glanced over his shoulder to the oncoming riders, now taking definite shape and form in the distance. He shook his head.

"I'm through bowing and scraping to Pride Seevert. Know I should have felt that way years ago but I was fool enough to string along with the rest of the people around here — or most of them. I'm making a change right here."

Dave cast a worried look toward the approaching horsemen. "Don't be a fool. You've got too much to lose. Take Hannah and get out of here before it's too late!"

"Too late," Bradford echoed bitterly. "Maybe I am late in admitting to myself how things are around here — but it ain't too late to change! Had me a real, first-class look at Pride Seevert and how he does things there this morning and it fair turned my stomach to realize I've had a part in letting him get away with it . . . If it's all the same with you, I'll stick."

"Up to you," Keegan said. "We can use another gun, but you ought to know the chances are plenty slim."

"I figure they'll be pretty good," the rancher said, looking toward the rocky slope of the mountain. "Half a dozen men could hold off a fair-sized army up there."

"Well, we better be high-tailin' for them rocks, or we'll never get the chance!" Pete Weems said in a worried voice.

The old puncher was right, Dave saw, glancing back down the trail. The Seeverts were closing the gap fast. He nodded to Bradford.

"We're glad to have you. . . . Maybe — if things go right — we can settle things once and for all with the Seeverts."

"Just what I'm hoping we can do," Bradford said, and turned to Hannah. "You get on down the trail for the Corrigans' girl. Don't worry none about me. We'll make it all right. Soon as this's over — "

"I'm not running either!" Hannah broke in flatly and drove spurs into her horse. The startled black she mounted spurted ahead, started up the slope at a fast gallop.

"Head her off!" Keegan shouted, jabbing

his own horse and waving the others forward. "Be no place for a woman up there when — "

A splatter of gunshots coming from their back trail cut off his words. He twisted about. The Seeverts were close — still out of bullet range, but close. Anger and frustration rushing through him, he turned to the others.

"Let her go! Too late now to do anything."

XVII

With Hannah a good fifty yards in the lead, they pounded up the rock-studded path. Raging inwardly, Dave kept his eyes on the girl's crouched figure. Her presence changed everything. He'd have to avoid an out and out showdown with Pride Seevert and his men now; he couldn't risk her getting hurt. . . . The little fool — didn't she realize what she was doing?

More shooting erupted from the Seevert party. Dave didn't trouble to look back; they were still well beyond range. Pete Weems, directly in front of him, turned.

"How high up we goin'?"

"Place about a mile farther on," Keegan shouted. "Trail bends left, goes by a rocky canyon. We'll fort up there."

The old puncher bobbed his head in understanding. He pointed to the girl. "What about her?"

"She'll double back when she sees us pull off the road." Temper again rolled through Keegan. "She dealt herself in on this. She'll have to look out for herself!"

Weems grinned, nodded again, and spurred forward to relay word of their destination to Henley and Cass Bradford. Dave twisted, looked to the rear. The Seven Diamond riders were now strung out in a long line on the lower portion of the trail. Pride Seevert was pushing them hard. Once they reached the rocky canyon, Dave realized, he and the others wouldn't have much time in which to get set.

The horses began to wilt under the steady climb. Keegan raised himself on the saddle and looked ahead. The bend in the trail was in sight. He drew his pistol, pointed it aloft and fired a single shot. Hannah glanced over her shoulder. He motioned to her to stop and she pulled in the black at once.

As they caught up with her Dave waved her in. "Stay close," he yelled, moving to the fore. "We're turning off."

Hannah nodded. Her eyes were bright with excitement and her lips were compressed to a tight line. Keegan wondered if she really understood what she had gotten herself into, or had any idea of what lay ahead for them. Likely not, he decided, anger once more stirring him.

Hannah Bradford would soon find out. The Seeverts weren't there for a Sunday picnic. His only hope, and worry, was that he could prevent her from getting hurt. He had a brief wonder at the possibility of Pride allowing her to leave before matters reached the critical stage.

Immediately he dismissed the thought; Pride Seevert would never agree — and if he did he could not be trusted to stand by his word. Like as not he would seize Hannah the moment she rode out, and use her as a hostage to gain a quick victory.

Dave reached the bend in the roadway, rounded it and urged the buckskin on toward the narrow mouth of the canyon a hundred yards farther on. Gaining the opening, he swung into it immediately. There was no identifiable trail. Only a maze of brush, boulders and stunted trees. The buckskin faltered on the rough terrain and Dave dropped from the saddle, motioned to the others to do likewise.

"That pile of rocks," he said, pointing to a jumbled mass of jagged granite and twisted junipers near dead center of the high-walled gash. "Be the best place."

Leading their horses, they struggled over the rough, uneven ground and moved in behind the natural fortification. Picketing their mounts in the deep brush beyond, they returned to the rocks.

Pete Weems glanced to the sheer palisades

rising on either side. "Sure ain't nobody goin' to be slippin' up on us from there," he said. "How about back of us?"

"Box canyon — runs for a mile or so," Keegan replied. "Only way they can get at us is from the front."

Pete grunted his satisfaction, moved to a place where he had a commanding view of the trail. "Might as well get ourselves sot. . . . Reckon Pride and the boys'll be along right soon now."

Dave only half heard. His gaze was on Hannah Bradford standing a few paces to one side with her father. The rancher caught his eye, smiled lamely.

"Sorry about this, Keegan. . . . Hannah just wasn't thinkin' — "

"Tried to figure a way to get you out of this," Dave said, placing his attention on the girl. His tone was angry, impatient. "Couldn't come up with an answer, so you'll have to stay."

"Don't make allowances for me," she said stiffly. "I can use a gun — as good as most men."

"You'll keep out of it!" Keegan snapped. "We're up against enough trouble without you getting yourself shot."

Hannah tossed her head angrily. "I'll do what I like!"

"The hell you will!" Keegan exploded, thoroughly aroused. "You'll do exactly what I tell you — or I'll stake you out with a rope. That stubborn streak of yours has already put us in a bad way — I won't have you making things worse!"

Startled, the girl stared at him. "I — I'll — "

"You'll listen and do what you're told. I want you back there with the horses. And you're to stay there. Understand?"

For a long moment Hannah faced him, defiant, strong-willed, and then she dropped her head. "I understand," she murmured, and wheeling, started for the brush where the horses had been picketed.

Dave brushed at the sweat clothing his face, glanced at Cass Bradford. The rancher was regarding him with a quiet smile.

"How you fixed for bullets?" Keegan asked.

Bradford ran one hand over his cartridge belt. "Couple dozen, more or less."

"Going to have to make every shot count if Pride means to make a fight of it."

"He will," the rancher said flatly. "Knows he's got us backed into a corner. Not like him to pass up a good chance. Anywhere special you want me?"

Dave shook his head. "Pick your own — "

"Here they come!" Pete Weems sang out.

"Now, you all harken to me — I got first claim on Pride. You hear? He's my meat."

"Forget it," Keegan said harshly. "Hold your fire until I give the word. Goes for everybody."

XVIII

Weems turned, his weathered face furrowed into a frown. "What's that mean?"

"Just what I said."

Pete continued to stare. "Thought you was out to settle with the Seeverts?"

"Aim to — only things have changed a bit."

"The girl — that it?"

"Could be," Dave replied, and let it drop.

"Then what're you figurin' to do?" Henley asked, shifting restlessly. "Make up your mind. They're gettin' close."

"Try talking Pride out of it. There'll come another time."

Weems swore in disgust. "Ain't never goin' to be a time good as this'n."

Keegan's attention was on the bend in the trail. Seevert and the men with him were just rounding the dark shoulder of rock, walking their horses slowly. Apparently they expected trouble.

Again Pete Weems swore, stirred irritably. The barrel of his rifle clanged against the rock he was crouching behind. Instantly Pride Seevert lifted his hand, halted.

Keegan flashed an angry look at Weems. He had planned to let the Seven Diamond riders advance until they were directly opposite — to where they would be within easy reach of their guns — but that advantage was lost now.

"Keegan!"

Pride Seevert's tone was impatient. Dave made no answer, hoping the men would continue. But the eldest Seevert was not to be fooled.

"Keegan — I know you're holed up in those rocks. I'm giving you one minute to come out — with your hands up!"

Dave edged forward to where he was partially visible. "We're holed up all right. What's more we've got every man with you covered. First one to make a wrong move is dead."

Seevert half rose in his stirrups, glanced over the riders clustered around him. He laughed. "Big talk when you figure the odds. There are a dozen of us!"

"But we're holding all the aces. Want to talk it over?"

"Why talk?"

"Because there's a rifle pointed at your belly, ready to go off when I give the word."

Pride Seevert relaxed gently. Chancy crowded in close, said something in a quick, anxious way. One of the riders behind him looked over his shoulder as if wishing he were nearer the protective shoulder of rock. Gabe Seevert, at Pride's immediate left, continued to slouch and wait.

"What's the deal, Keegan?"

"Couple of people here that're not mixed up in what's between us. Let them go."

"Sure. Tell them to ride out."

Dave laughed. "Your word's no good to me, Pride."

Again Chancy spoke hurriedly to his brother. Pride shook his head. "What are you wanting me to do, then?"

"Take your bunch on up the trail. Keep going for an hour — "

"And give you a chance to run?" Chancy broke in. "Hell, no!"

"I'm not running. I'll be around. Just want my friends out of it."

"Well, I sure ain't goin' no place," Weems grumbled. "You can tell 'em that for me!"

"That mean you'll be waiting when we come back?" Pride asked.

"I'll be here."

Seevert shrugged. "You won't take my word, but you want me to take yours."

"About the size of it," Dave answered.

He was pushing his luck, he knew, but he was trying hard to prevent a standoff — a standoff that would eventually erupt in gunfire. Without Hannah on his hands he would not hesitate to take on Seevert and his men. Well entrenched in the rocks he, with Pete Weems and Joe Henley, could more than even the odds; but with the girl — and her father who likely would prove more a liability than an asset — he had to avoid a shootout.

Pride Seevert's voice brought him from his thoughts. "What if I say no?"

"You'd be a fool. . . . You don't have much choice."

"Could make a run for the rocks. . . ."

"Maybe half of you'd make it. Probably less."

Seevert made an angry, frustrated gesture. "All right! Dcal is we ride on, double back in one hour. You'll be here."

"He won't be by hisself!" Pete Weems yelled suddenly, springing to his feet. "Damn you to hell, Pride Seevert! Had my way, I'd cut loose on the whole passel of you right now!"

Seevert stared at the trembling figure of the old man. After a time he shook his head.

"Who else you got up there, Keegan?"

"Don't see as it matters." A thought came

to Dave. "You want to keep this strictly between us — just you and me?"

"Meaning?"

"Send your men on. I'll do the same with the people with me. Then you and I can settle this alone."

"Why not?"

Cass Bradford came about, his features strained. "You ain't thinking of doing that, are you?" he asked incredulously. "You'd be a plain fool!"

"I'm looking for a way out of this — any way at all," Dave said grimly. "We haven't got a prayer if they decide to wait us out."

"But — "

"Thing I'm interested in is getting Hannah and you in the clear. Goes for Pete and Henley, too, if they're of a mind."

"I ain't lookin' to pull out," Weems declared. "Don't figure Joe'll be, either — but you're plumb loco if you make a bargain like that with Pride."

"Pete's right," Bradford said. "Pride'll never face up to you alone. If he don't ambush you, he'll have his whole bunch standin' by, ready to cut you down."

"Have to figure on that," Keegan said.

Weems groaned. Bradford wagged his head helplessly.

"Where you want to meet?" Pride called.

Keegan considered. Important thing was to keep the Bradfords out of it. Seevert evidently was unaware of their being with him — and it should be kept that way in event the showdown backfired.

"Hell Canyon," Dave said, choosing a point well distant and in the opposite direction. "You've got a liking for the place."

"Suits me. When?"

"This afternoon. . . . Say three o'clock."

Pride nodded. "I'll be there. What guarantee I got that you'll show?"

"My word — and I don't go back on it."

Seevert stirred indifferently. "Won't make no difference. If you don't I can still hunt you down. It all right if we move out?"

"Go ahead — up the trail. Any of your bunch turns back I'll figure the deal's off and start shooting."

Seevert turned, said something to the men behind him. Chancy protested but Pride waved him to silence, put his horse into motion. In single file the riders fell in line.

"Sure a mistake," Pete Weems muttered, squinting at the procession. "We had them skunks by the short hair. Should've blowed them off the map!"

Henley released the hammers on his shotgun, reached for his plug of tobacco. "Had

133

old Pride stopped cold, sure enough, else he wouldn't have been so agreeable. You really goin' up there and havin' it out with him?"

Dave nodded as he continued to watch the departing riders. "Nothing's changed, far as the Seeverts are concerned."

Bradford looked down. "Reckon it was my fault — me and my daughter's — that you lost a good chance. I'm obliged to you for thinkin' of her — but don't go counting me out. Done made up my mind about Pride and his bunch and I ain't drawing a full breath until I see them crawlin'."

Keegan turned to the rancher as hope pushed through him. "Cass, there a chance you could talk some of the others into seeing things your way? They wouldn't listen to me."

Bradford rose, holstered his weapon, "Might be a couple — Ed Corrigan for one, Ollie Miller for another. Maybe more. Why? What're you thinkin'?"

"I'm not fool enough to believe Pride'll be at Hell Canyon alone — but I still aim to meet him like I promised. Occurred to me that if you and some of the other ranchers came along — not with me but behind me — we might get this problem settled for everybody."

"See what you mean," Henley said, catching on quickly. "We can bank on Pride ringin' in his outfit once you show up, but if he sees a bunch of the ranchers standin' by, backin' your play — "

Dave prodded Bradford gently. "What do you think?"

"Sure as hell worth a try," the rancher said. He glanced to the sun. "Ain't got much time, however. Expect I'd better be ridin' if I aim to do much talkin'."

Keegan's shoulders relaxed slightly. Perhaps the end of Pride Seevert's rule over Tenkiller Flats was in sight after all.

"Good," he said, "and this time lock that daughter of yours in a room somewhere so she won't get in the way," he added with a grin.

"I'll do that," Bradford said. "Where'll we meet?"

Dave looked off to the north. "Hell Canyon."

XIX

Bradford studied Dave closely as if uncertain of his hearing. Then he shrugged. "Could be crowdin' things a mite," he said, "but I reckon you know what you're doin'."

Joe Henley shifted his double-barrel from right hand to left. "He's maybe got somethin' there. Might be smart to sort of hold back, see who all's comin' to the party."

"Was me who set the time," Keegan said. "Means that's when I'll be there."

Complete silence followed Dave's words, broken finally by Bradford.

"You're calling the shots," the rancher said, and started for the horses.

Keegan motioned to Henley. "Take a look up the trail — see if the Seeverts are sticking to the agreement."

The older man nodded, moved out of the rocks toward the path. Dave turned, and with Pete Weems at his heels, followed Bradford to where the mounts were picketed.

Hannah was already in the saddle when they reached the brush. She passed the reins of her father's horse to him, smiled down at Keegan.

"I'm sorry," she said contritely. "I didn't realize I was going to ruin things for you."

"It'll work out," Dave said gruffly. "Maybe better."

"I hope so."

He glanced up, met her eyes. She was smiling softly. "Good luck," she murmured. "I'll be — "

"Come on, girl!" Cass Bradford broke in. "Got to get movin' if I'm to make all them calls."

He pulled away at once and Hannah, with a final smile at Dave, swung in behind him. Keegan looked toward the trail. Joe Henley had his arm up, signaling that all was in order.

Keegan knew it would not be otherwise. Pride Seevert figured the meeting at Hell Canyon would be a cinch deal — all his way. He wouldn't risk queering it with a false move now. And Pride *would* have it all his way unless he could come up with a good idea, Dave thought, stepping up to the buckskin. So far everything had worked fine: he had been able to get Hannah and Cass Bradford out of the way before a shot was fired — and without the Seeverts being aware of their presence.

Next would be the confrontation at Hell Canyon — and a plan of some sort that would afford him at least an even chance of coming out alive. He would, of course, like nothing better than a showdown with Pride Seevert alone, but Pride didn't operate that way. The eldest Seevert would start things off, then leave it to his brothers or his hired guns to finish.

He went to the buckskin's saddle, delayed while Pete Weems mounted and gathered in the reins of Henley's horse. When the old puncher was settled, he wheeled about and headed for the trail slowly.

Weems said, "Where's Joe and me fit in this?"

"Still feel like cutting yourself in?"

"You're dang right — leastwise I do!" Pete answered. "Ain't nothin' changed."

They reached the trail, halted. Henley crossed to his horse, climbed stiffly to the saddle. To his right Dave could see the figures of the Bradfords diminishing into the distance. To the left the way was clear; the Seeverts were out of sight. He heard Weems speak.

"Joe, you still comin' along?"

"Wouldn't miss this here hoedown for a peck of money," the old man replied. "Where we goin' now?"

Dave realized the question was directed

to him. He glanced to the north. "Just thinking about a ledge up near the canyon. On
the west side of the mountain; sort of over-
looks everything below. Be a good place to
watch the Seeverts from."

"That'd be a right smart thing to do,"
Weems said, bobbing his head vigorously.
"Get us an idea of what old Pride's plannin'
to pull. But how we goin' to get there without
them spottin' us?"

"Trail forks about half a mile on up, swings
to the other side of the mountain. If we
follow it we can come in from behind, and
be above them. . . . Long ride but we've
got plenty of time."

"How long?" Henley asked.

"Couple hours, maybe little more. Why?"

"Was just thinkin' we could use a bite to
eat. Never did get around to that breakfast
I cooked up this mornin'. You figure it might
be a good idea for me to drop back to your
place and get us some vittles?"

"I'm for that!" Pete Weems said. "My
guts is growlin' somethin' fierce. Reckon it's
'cause I'm hungry. How about you, Dave?"

It dawned on Keegan then that he, too,
was in need of a meal. He had eaten little
that previous night and, like the others, had
been interrupted before he could touch his
food that morning.

"Go ahead," he said. "We'll leave a marker on the trail showing you where to turn off for the ledge."

"I'll find it," Henley said, and wheeled about. "Adios."

"Adios — and don't you be takin' all day!" Weems said. "This here shindig comes off at three o'clock sharp!"

"I'll be there," Henley shouted as he put his horse to a lope.

Keegan and Weems moved off up the trail. They rode in silence the short distance to where a faint path led off the main course and cut its steep way up the slope.

"Goin' to be mean," the old puncher said, eyeing the area critically. "Way it looks everything's been washed out."

"If it has," Dave answered, "we'll make a new one."

They clambered over a rock slide, broke out onto smoothly washed ground. Dave looked up-slope and pointed to a low butte.

"Trail goes around that bluff. I remember it now."

"I'd say you ain't the only one rememberin'," Pete Weems commented in a low voice.

Keegan looked back. The old puncher was staring at the ground, his features sober.

"Them's fresh tracks."

Dave dropped from the saddle, squatted

over the hoof-prints pressed into the smooth soil. They were no more than an hour old, if that. Rising, he probed the country before him carefully; there was no horseman in sight.

But there was a man up there, somewhere — one dispatched by Pride Seevert. That meant Pride knew about the ledge, that he was stationing one of his gunmen there as an additional precaution.

"This could be Pride's ace in the hole," he said half aloud. "He'll make a show of sending all the rest of his bunch away, but all the time he'll have this jasper on the ledge looking down on me over his rifle sights."

"Sounds like Pride, sure enough," Weems said dryly.

Keegan stepped back onto the buckskin, eyes still on the lifting slope. "Don't think whoever it is up there will be looking for us on his back trail, but we won't gamble on it. Keep it quiet and stay behind me."

Weems for once had no comment, simply followed orders. They climbed the grade slowly, approaching the butte at an angle that closed them off from view of anyone beyond it.

Reaching that point Dave signaled a halt, and again dismounting, made his way to the flat-crested bulge of rock. Keeping low, he worked around to the opposite side. The trail, definite and unmarred by storms, stretched out before him toward the rim of the mountain. He could see no one moving along its winding course.

Dropping back to Weems he reported his findings, adding, "We'll stay to the side — in the brush. Be harder going, but nobody'll see us."

The old puncher grinned tightly. "Sort of gives a man a creepy feelin' knowin' somebody's up ahead just waitin' for a chance to put a bullet in his brisket."

"He won't get the chance if we're careful," Dave said.

"Sound carries a far piece up in the hills like this."

"Doubt if he'll be listening or watching. Pride gave him orders to get on that ledge and lay low. That's all he'll be thinking about."

"And Pride'll be figurin' on him bein' there — a bush-whacker all cocked and primed to cut down on you when he gives the high-sign."

"Just about the way it's set up," Keegan said, and added, "Wonder if he's the same one who took those shots at me at my place that first day?"

Pete Weems looked down. "That was me,"

he said in a low voice.

Keegan whirled on his saddle. "You! Why in the . . . ?"

"Was afeerd you'd change your mind once you seen your place and keep on goin'. Wanted to make you mad enough to stay and fight the Seeverts. Figured throwin' a couple a shots at you from the brush'd do that."

Dave, over his surprise, smiled wryly. "Guess it worked."

"Maybe so — only I can see now there weren't no need. I'm plumb sorry, Dave."

"Forget it," Keegan said. "Let's get to that ledge and take care of a real bush-whacker. Think maybe this time Pride Seevert's outsmarted himself."

XX

Around noon they paused to rest in the shade of a wind-tipped juniper. They were just below the rim and less than a quarter mile, Dave estimated, from the shelf of rock; but the horses were blowing from the stiff climb and lathered with sweat.

Weems, sprawled full-length, looked off down the long slope and mopped at his face. "Sure wishin' Joe'd turn up with that grub . . . powerful hungry. . . ."

Dave Keegan had thought little more of food after the ascent of the mountain had begun. His mind was on the Seeverts and what lay ahead. He had gone into the situation glowing with anger at the injustice being dispensed by the owners of Seven Diamond. This became more intense when they endeavored to force him into line with the other ranchers, but when he had learned that his father had also suffered the brutal pressure of the Seevert brothers, the fires within him had leaped to a high pitch.

Now the time of reckoning was at hand;

a reckoning he had, perhaps, deliberately pro-voked. Dave had no liking for what faced him — death for Pride Seevert and possibly for himself — but he was a man who knew that such a problem must be met head-on and settled definitely, once and for all.

Only the end of the Seeverts would write finish to the trouble on Tenkiller Flats, but he wished there were another answer besides a gun; there was no glory in killing, only a revolting sickness, yet he knew he had no choice. It was the only thing Pride and his brothers understood and thus the only means by which their grip on the country could be broken. Still, if he talked to Pride, gave him a chance to pull out . . .

He stared up at the cloudless sky, gleaming blue through the heat. Two vultures high overhead dipped and soared on broad, tireless wings. *Waiting,* he thought, *just waiting.*

"Reckon we ought to be movin'?"

Pete Weems's question jarred him. He nod-ded, got to his feet and walked to the buckskin. Halting next to the horse he glanced to the rim above them.

"Up on top," he said, "the trail forks. The one going straight on leads to the ledge. Other one follows the ridge for a spell, then drops off."

Weems said, "You figurin' we ought to

part, come in on the ledge from two sides?"

"Be the smart way to do it. You take the ridge. Best we go quiet — and no shooting. Don't want Pride and the rest to know something's wrong."

The old puncher signified his understanding. "What about the horses?"

"We'll leave them on the ridge."

Pete groaned softly. "Never was much for walkin'."

"Be only a couple of hundred yards."

Weems grumbled something, climbed onto his saddle. Dave mounted, and again keeping to the brush, much sparser at the higher elevation, pressed on.

The buckskin broke out onto the top of the slope and walked slowly down into a small, grassy basin. Dave halted, waited for the old man to appear. A moment later Weems came over the edge and drew up near Keegan. They sat in silence, letting their tired horses graze for a time, and then Dave pointed to a rocky pathway leading on to the north.

"Stay on that. It'll cut to your right just beyond those cedars and take you down to the ledge. Leave your horse there and double back. Expect we'll find our bushwhacker somewhere near the middle."

Pete said, "I savvy. . . . One thing — if

you get there first, be mighty careful. Them snakes Pride hires can be plenty tricky."

"Same goes for you," Keegan replied and headed across the basin.

He would reach the shelf first — he had planned it that way. Not that he didn't trust the old puncher; he simply believed it was his job and he wanted no man assuming a risk rightfully his.

Keegan gained the far side, found himself in a dense stand of scrub oak. Wishing to avoid noise, he veered right, circled the irregular patch and entered a grove of towering ponderosa pine. Halting there, he picketed the buckskin in a shady hollow where grass was plentiful. The ledge was dead ahead, below and beyond a ragged hogback.

Moving quietly he crossed to the rocky spine, picking his way with utmost care. One click of a stone, he knew, would alert the man now somewhere close by. A moment later he saw a blur of motion, froze. It was a horse, tied well back in the brush that covered the ledge.

Knowing the rider would not be far away, Dave dropped to his belly, wormed to the face of the hogback and looked over.

Gabe Seevert, rifle across his lap, sat near the edge of the shelf, smoking a cigarette. He was turned sideways to Keegan.

Dave studied the land briefly and then withdrew. Dropping to a point some thirty or forty feet below the man, he again made his way to the ridge. Glancing over, he gave a grunt of satisfaction; Gabe's broad back was now to him.

The problem was getting down to the ledge unheard. Keegan mulled that puzzle about in his mind, spurred by the need to get the matter handled before Pete Weems came onto the scene, and came to a hurried decision. Sitting down, he removed his boots, hooked them under his belt and began a slow, crawling descent of the embankment.

Reaching the bottom without incident, he paused, stifling his labored breathing. The sound of voices coming up from the clearing adjacent to the canyon was clear. Dave gave thanks for that; Gabe, not suspecting anyone was behind him, was keeping his attention on the men below.

Drawing his pistol, Dave drew himself to a crouch and catfooted it to where the man sat.

"Don't move!" he warned, jamming the muzzle of the weapon into Gabe's thick neck.

Seevert stiffened with shock and surprise. The cigarette fell from his lips.

"Who — "

"Not a sound!" Keegan snapped, throwing

the rifle aside. "Start scooting back from the edge, quiet!"

Immediately Gabe began to hitch his way from the lip of the shelf. He still had not caught a glimpse of his captor and he continually tried to see from the corner of his eye while beads of sweat thickened on his ruddy face. Well back from possible view below, Dave stopped.

"Far enough," he said. "Now sit until my partner gets here."

Gabe Seevert sighed heavily in relief. He twisted his head around. His eyes widened.

"Keegan — where in the hell . . . ?"

"Maybe you're forgetting I grew up in this country," Dave said. "Knew about this ledge, too."

Gabe's shoulders went down. He shook his head. "Always figured things'd blow sky-high someday. Kept tellin' Pride that — only he wouldn't listen."

Keegan glanced to the north. Pete Weems had reached the fringe of brush at the end of the ledge, was peering at him questioningly. Dave waved him in.

"Maybe you should've talked harder," he said.

Gabe frowned. "You aim to shoot him down from here?"

Anger rushed through Keegan. "That's

what you were sent up here for — to put a bullet in me, wasn't it? Where's the difference?"

Gabe dropped his head. "Was Pride's idea."

"But you went along with it. You could — "

"You got him! By God, it's Gabe!" Pete Weems exclaimed, coming in crouched low.

"Yeah, it's Gabe," Dave said. "All set to pick me off like we figured." He pointed to the brush at the lower end of the ledge. "Saw his horse down there. See if he's carrying a rope. This is one Seevert that's not going to do much moving around rest of the day."

Weems hurried off. Dave reached down, plucked Gabe's pistol from its holster, thrust it under his own belt. Gabe watched him steadily, suspiciously.

"What're you goin' to do?"

"Not hang you — I'll leave that to somebody else. I'm just tying you up."

Keegan was suddenly conscious of the quiet below in the clearing. Shortly Pride Seevert's voice sounded.

"Gabe — you ready up there?"

Dave shoved the gun barrel deeper into Seevert's flabby neck. "Answer him, damn you!" he said savagely. "And you better say the right words or this war'll start right here with me blowing your head off!"

XXI

Gabe Seevert swallowed hard. "All set," he croaked.

There was a brief silence and then Pride's voice, suppressed and irritable, came again. "What's the matter with you?"

Keegan pressed harder. Gabe flinched. "I'm all right!" he shouted desperately. "Everything's fine!"

"Well, keep your eyes peeled," Pride said, satisfied. "Keegan'll be showing up pretty soon."

Immediately, the murmur of voices resumed below. Dave relented, lowered his arm. "Keep playing it smart," he said, settling back, "and maybe you'll live to see the next sunrise."

Pete Weems trotted up carrying a coiled lariat over his shoulder. Keegan motioned Gabe to a stump at the extreme rear of the ledge and directed him to sit beside it.

After they had bound and gagged the man securely, Dave and Weems returned to the edge of the shelf and, lying flat, looked down on the clearing. Pride Seevert, with Chancy close by, was sitting on a large rock. Gathered around them, some squatting on their heels, others taking their ease full-length, were nine of their hired hands.

Pride was just concluding a story of some sort and all were laughing. Pete Weems shifted angrily.

"Mighty sure of hisself."

Seevert could hardly be otherwise, Dave thought. He'd had everything his way for so long that he had no comprehension of opposition, much less of defeat.

"What's the time?" he asked in a hushed voice.

The old puncher dug about in his pocket until he produced a thick, nickeled watch. " 'Most half past one."

Over an hour to wait. Keegan rolled to his back, glanced toward the spine of rock. He, too, was feeling hunger and wishing Joe Henley would put in an appearance.

And the ranchers. There was no sign of them — not even of Cass Bradford. He stifled his impatience. There'd scarcely been time enough yet; give them another hour. Anyway, there was no assurance they would come; like Pride Seevert, except in reverse, they had been dominated by a ruthless power for so long they'd forgotten how to resist.

The minutes dragged. Weems dozed, as an old man will, in the hot sun. Gabe Seevert twisted and turned, seeking comfort that could not be found. Up on the rocks two striped chipmunks scampered about, eventually drawing the attention of a piñon jay who came to stare at them with beady eyes from behind his black mask. . . . Where the hell was Henley? Had he, somehow, missed the turnoff on the trail? He should —

"You boys better get moving." Pride Seevert's words reached Keegan clearly. "Don't want to scare our rabbit off before he comes to the snare."

Chancy laughed. "You reckon you're goin' to be safe, big brother?"

"I'm always safe," Pride answered and also laughed. "Sort of a rule of mine."

Dave watched the Seven Diamond riders rouse, stroll leisurely to their horses and mount, Chancy leading them. When all were in the saddle Pride stepped to his younger brother's side. There was no levity in his manner now.

"You sure you got things right?"

Chancy frowned. "Course I have!" he replied in an injured tone. "What the hell — you'd think I didn't have a lick of sense!"

Pride made no comment, simply wheeled and returned to the rock. He sat down,

153

watched Chancy and the others ride slowly out of the clearing and up the trail.

Up the trail.

Keegan's eyes narrowed as he gave that thought. If Chancy and his men intended to return to Seven Diamond headquarters they would have taken an opposite direction. To the north lay the higher levels of Tenkiller Mountain, and little else. There were a few game trails, he recalled, that dropped off and wound through the arroyos and lesser canyons to the flats, but no man was likely to choose such a rugged route intentionally.

It could mean only one thing: they weren't actually leaving.

Back in his mind Keegan had known all along that Pride Seevert would devise such a plan; he simply hadn't given it any consideration. Undoubtedly Chancy and his followers would draw off a short distance, hide in the brush or possibly one of the many side draws that slashed the area. There they would be at Pride's call every moment.

Dave grinned tightly. The eldest Seevert left nothing to chance; not only had he stationed Gabe above on the ledge where he had absolute control of the clearing, but he also was positioning Chancy and nine of his hired guns where they would be handy.

It wasn't going to be easy. Danger from

Gabe had been removed but Chancy and his crowd posed a serious problem. He would be forced to depend more on Pete Weems than he had intended — and on Joe Henley, if only he'd return. The wiry old man and his shotgun would really be a big help.

Weems stirred, muttered something unintelligible. Dave reached over, shook him gently.

"Time?"

"Quarter past two," the old puncher replied, fumbling with the heavy piece. "Anythin' happen?"

"Chancy and the boys rode out — north."

"North? Where they goin' that way?"

"Expect Pride's got them hiding out nearby."

Pete swore. "That'd be him, all right."

Keegan drew back from the edge and sat up. Pulling his pistol he checked the cylinder for loads, then returned it to its leather pocket.

"I'll be going," he said. "Take me a little while to circle around, come in by the trail."

Weems frowned, looked to the lower end of the clearing. "Seen anything of Bradford and them folks he was bringin'?"

"Not yet."

"By dingies, they'd better be comin'! This here ruckus is all for them."

"Better not figure on it," Dave said. "Comes right down to it, it's my fight."

"No more'n theirs!"

"Maybe, but they were willing to go along with the Seeverts. I wasn't — and that drops it in my lap."

Weems cast an angry, sidelong glance at Gabe slumped against the stump. "Well, don't you be forgettin' I'm in it!"

"I'm not. I'm figuring on you staying put right up here. If things get out of hand I'll holler, and you cut yourself in. Otherwise, leave it up to me."

"You ain't thinkin' you got a chance against the whole bunch, are you?"

"Pride won't call in Chancy unless he has to — and long as he's sure Gabe's sitting up here with a rifle on my back, he won't. I'm going to try and settle things with him before it comes to that."

"Comes to what?"

"Shooting. . . ."

Pete's jaw sagged. "You mean you're goin' to try and talk sense . . . ?"

Dave nodded, got to his feet. Keeping low, he started for the end of the shelf.

"You're a plumb fool!" Weems said in genuine alarm. "You'll be handin' Pride the chance he'll be lookin' for. . . . I know him!"

"So do I," Keegan said quietly. "Keep a sharp watch, and be careful. Want Pride to think Gabe's still up here, ready."

The old puncher mumbled a dissatisfied reply that was lost to Dave as he moved into the brush and began a slow, cautious descent to the clearing.

He reached it half an hour later, coming in at a point fifty feet or so below where Pride Seevert was waiting. Halting behind a thick stand of mountain mahogany, he turned his head to the trail and listened. He could hear nothing that would indicate the approach of Bradford and any of the ranchers he had succeeded in enlisting to the cause; Dave swung his attention again to the eldest Seevert.

Pride had forsaken the rock and was now upright and lighting a slim, black cigar. He drew in deeply, exhaled a cloud of smoke and watched it drift lazily away. Coming around then, he looked up to the ledge.

"Gabe!"

His voice was soft as though he were making certain it would carry only a short distance. He rode out several seconds and when there was no reply he repeated the summons more insistently. Worry lifted within Dave. If Gabe made no answer . . .

"Yeah?"

Keegan felt relief trickle through him. He grinned faintly. Pete Weems's imitation was surprisingly close.

"What the hell's the matter with you — you sleeping up there?"

"Nope. Just waitin'."

Pride was satisfied. "All right. Time's about up. Keegan ought to be showing — if he's going to."

Dave touched the butt of the pistol at his hip, took a long breath. "I'm here," he said, and stepped into the open.

XXII

In the sudden hush Pride Seevert stood absolutely motionless for the space of several breaths. Then, with great deliberateness, he reached for the cigar clenched between his teeth and removed it. Smoke trickled from the corners of his mouth.

"Thought you'd be smarter than this, Keegan."

Dave closed in slowly, step at a time. "Said I'd be here."

"Yeah, guess you did. Makes things easy for me."

"Maybe, but before you start anything you'd better listen — hear me out."

Pride watched Keegan ease into within a dozen paces, halt. "I'm through talking, nothing more to be said."

"Could be worth your life — "

"Doubt that, but go ahead."

"This is going to end in a killing — one or could be both of us. I'm offering you the chance to call it off, ride out of this country, take your brothers."

"You what?" Seevert exclaimed in amazement.

"You heard me. You're through here on the Flats, one way or another."

"Me — walk off — leave everything? Hell, I own this country, Keegan! It's mine, lock, stock and water bucket!"

"Not any more."

Pride Seevert stared at Keegan, finally began to laugh. "Beats all," he said, shaking his head. "You telling me to move on — you! What makes you think you're big enough?"

"One thing — you're going to decide here and now. There's just the two of us, and either you agree to pull out, or you reach for that gun you're wearing. It's that simple."

"Not quite. I've — "

"No. Gabe's not up there on the ledge with a rifle. He can't give you any help. And if you sing out for Chancy, I'll kill you."

At Dave's flat, quiet words Pride Seevert froze. Color began to drain from his face. He threw a hasty glance toward the shelf of rock.

"I — I don't believe a goddam thing you're saying," he managed.

Dave shrugged. "Pete," he called, "show yourself!"

He came to stunned attention as the voice of Joe Henley reached him.

"Things is all right up here, Mr. Seevert. . . . You go right ahead. I'll turn Gabe loose in a minute. Dassen't take my eyes off'n Pete here just yet."

Relief crossed Pride's features, and the old confidence returned. "Joe's working for me again," he said. "Hired him back when he came out and told me he was signing up with you. Figured he'd be useful."

The shock of being double-crossed faded into anger within Dave Keegan. He looked to the ledge. Weems was upright, arms aloft. Henley, shotgun muzzle pressed into the old puncher's back, was standing warily behind him. Keegan smiled grimly. With Henley thus occupied Pride was little better off.

"Still makes it you and me," he said. "What's it to be? You pulling out or — "

"The hell with you!" Seevert yelled, and jumped for the protection of the rock. "Chancy!"

Dave drew fast, snapped a bullet at Pride. He threw himself to one side as Seevert fired an answering shot, winced as the slug plucked at his sleeve. He tried for a second time at Pride but Seevert was crouched low and offered no target.

Then, beyond the rock, Dave saw Chancy

161

and his riders burst from the trees and charge into the clearing.

Tight lipped, Keegan rushed for the brush to his left. He heard Pride yell, saw him rise and level his pistol. Dave triggered instinctively. Pride jolted, staggered back and fell against the rock. More yells lifted as Chancy and the Seven Diamond riders pounded in. Guns began to crackle through the rising dust and smoke. Dave felt a solid smash against his leg, went down. Dirt spurted over him.

He threw two shots at the oncoming horsemen, rolled frantically to get further into the brush. He caught a glimpse of Chancy Seevert out in front, bearing down upon him. Pulling himself up slightly, he emptied his gun at Chancy, saw him buckle and fall from the saddle as his frightened horse veered off sharply.

Fighting the searing pain in his leg, Keegan fumbled at his belt for cartridges with which to reload. He paused, suddenly aware of the quiet. Drawing himself upright slowly, painfully, he glanced to the clearing where the spinning dust was beginning to settle. Seevert's riders were sitting motionless, hands above their heads.

Dave shifted his eyes to the opposite direction. Cass Bradford, Corrigan and two men he didn't know were advancing slowly. Each held a leveled rifle. Well beyond them he saw a fifth figure — Hannah.

Keegan finished reloading and hobbled into the open. Bradford grinned at him hurriedly, then swung his attention back to the Seven Diamond riders.

"Drop them guns — all of you!"

There was a series of thuds as the men complied. From above on the ledge Pete Weems's voice sounded.

"Bring 'em down here."

"What about Dave — he all right?"

Moving deeper into the clearing, Keegan looked up. "I'm fine. You?"

The old puncher waved. "Nothin' wrong with me a shot o' rye won't cure. What'll I do with these two skunks?"

"Pride's dead," Ed Corrigan said, coming up. "So's Chancy. Where's Gabe?"

"Up with Pete, tied to a stump. You got here just in time . . . obliged."

"Seems the thanks better go to you," Bradford said. "Big favor you done us all — even them that wasn't in on it." He paused, ducked his head toward the captive Seven Diamond men. "What'll we do with them?"

Dave leaned against the rock, favoring his throbbing leg. "Turn them loose, long as they promise to get out of the country, and stay out. Just hired hands."

"Could hold them for a trial."

"You've got Gabe to answer for anything you want to bring up."

"Figure that'll be plenty, once we have a look at what's in the bottom of Hell Canyon," Corrigan said.

Bradford nodded and grinned at Keegan, who was looking past his shoulder at Hannah, now entering the clearing.

"Tried to make her stay home but she wouldn't listen. Said most likely some of us would need doctorin'."

"Guess she was right," Dave agreed. "And I reckon I'm her first patient."